Foreign Words

FOREIGN WORDS

by Vassilis Alexakis

translated from the French
by Alyson Waters

AB
Autumn Hill Books
Iowa City, Iowa

*Æ*B

http://www.autumnhillbooks.com

Autumn Hill Books, Iowa City, Iowa 52240
© 2006 by Autumn Hill Books
All Right Reserved. Published 2006
Printed in the United States of America

Originally Published as *Les mots étrangers*
© 2002 by Éditions Stock

*Cet ouvrage, publié dans le cadre d'un programme d'aide à
la publication, beneficie du soutien du Ministère des Affaires
Étrangères et du Service Culturel de l'Ambassade de France aux
États-Unis.*

This work, published as part of a program of aid for publica-
tion, received support from the French Ministry of Foreign
Affairs and the Cultural Services of the French Embassy in the
United States.

Library of Congress Control Number: 2005933428

Autumn Hill Books ISBN-13: 978-0-9754444-1-2
Autumn Hill Books ISBN-10: 0-9754444-1-7

Acknowledgments from the Translator

I would like to thank Vassilis Alexakis — for writing this book, and for his kindness and encouragement during the translation process; the National Endowment for the Arts, whose support made this translation possible; Russell Valentino, for believing in this project from the start; Liz McGill, for designing a beautiful cover from the heart, and for reading my first draft; Elizabeth Fox, for her thoughtful reading and comments; Constance Waters, for listening to me read aloud; Elmer Waters, for introducing me to my first foreign words; and Margot and Gwenaël Kerlidou, for their patience and love. *Singila mingi.*

for Magda

1

The first word of Sango I learned was *baba*, "papa." It's easy to remember, of course. "My father" is translated as *baba ti mbi*. The possessive adjective "my" apparently doesn't exist in Sango, for *baba ti mbi* literally means "the father of me." *Kodoro* means both "village" and "country." If I had to say something about my identity, I would say, "*Kodoro ti mbi* is Greece."

Is there a word in Sango for Greece? But I don't want to talk about me (I repeat, *mbi*). I think I have exhausted the subject of my comings and goings between Athens and Paris. I realize in fact that it has become oppressively commonplace: several flights a day link the two capitals, and they're almost always full. And I don't feel like inventing a story. I suppose I should, for my published novels are so few and far between. I must admit, translating my own works from Greek into French or French into Greek takes so much time. My bibliography would surely be more extensive if I had not written each of my books twice.

These last few months I've had no ideas for a novel. Was I discouraged by *The Tin Soldier's* lukewarm, not to say cold (*de*, in Sango) reception last year? The adventures of Martine, the book's heroine (a little girl in love with a toy soldier) had been so moving to me, and I thought my readers would be moved as well. Alas, this was not the case.

"Your book came out either too early or too late," my publisher said as he gazed absent-mindedly out the window. "The French don't feel like crying this year."

The Tin Soldier will be published in Greek at the end of the year, with the same title (*O Molyvénios stratiotis*). I made several changes to the novel as I translated it. I got rid of quite a few sentences and abridged Martine's interior monologue in the basement of the Galeries Lafayette. By rereading myself through the lens of another language, I see my weaknesses more clearly, I correct them, and this explains why I prefer to be read in translation rather than in the original. I hope my compatriots will have a more positive reaction to the story. But perhaps they don't feel like crying either.

Only one idea has occurred to me since I finished this translation: to learn a new language. At first the project struck me as absurd. What did I need a third language for? I recalled all the trouble I had gone to at twenty-four to learn French, and all the difficulties I had come up against to regain fluency in my mother tongue some ten years later. I went even further back in time, to when my mother was teaching me the Greek alphabet. I had such a hard time recognizing the letters. My mother was despondent. She realized very early on that I had no gift for languages. I learned almost no English all those years I studied it in school.

Still, I couldn't get the idea out of my head. So perhaps I needed to admit to myself that it made some sense, had some meaning? Did I want to prove to myself that, at fifty-two, I was still young enough to learn something new? Whenever you begin to study a new language, you inevitably seem a bit foolish, you become a child again. Was I nostalgic for that time in my life when I didn't yet know how to speak? I had had no end of trouble getting the hang of French, but the effort had not been devoid of charms. Some of the words I encountered were so delightful to me, and I would enthusiastically try combining them in different ways to form sentences. The French language has become less amusing since it has become the tool with which I earn my so-called living. It's no longer a foreign language; I learned it so long ago that I have the impression I've always known how to speak it. Maybe I wanted to learn a foreign language simply because I didn't know any.

The project continued to ripen in my unconscious. One morning I woke up thinking about Africa. "I'll learn a little-known African language," I thought. This was yet another surprise, for I know hardly anything about Africa. I had been interested in it only as a child and teenager. I was aware that periodically it experienced dreadful tragedies, but I really never thought about it. I was content simply to boycott oranges from South Africa. My ignorance prevented me from striking up conversations with the Africans I'd meet in Paris or Athens. What was the point of asking them where they were from if I couldn't even locate their country on a map? Each African I'd encounter would add another layer of mystery to my confusion and embarrassment. What was behind this sudden interest in black culture? And why had I thought about a minor language? Was it so that my endeavor would be more unique? Because I felt compassion for those small languages that are having more and more difficulty making themselves heard? Greek was an endangered language as well.

The books and films from my childhood had described Africa as the crossroad of every imaginable danger. Tarzan had to be ever vigilant. He had a few friends—an elephant that was his means of transportation, a monkey that made faces at him (Tarzan would laugh from time to time)—yet he lived under the constant threat of ferocious animals and cannibalistic warriors. These warriors spoke in a rudimentary language that just barely allowed them to elaborate their diabolical schemes. Most of the white men who ventured into the jungle were slave traders and elephant slaughterers.

Yet Africa enchanted me. Instead of the narrow little world I inhabited, it offered me a free space where everything remained to be invented, everything was still possible. No other continent stimulated my imagination in this way. It was an amazing playground. I perceived Tarzan's famous cry as a hymn to freedom. I dreamed of sleeping on a bed of leaves. The lion that roared at the beginning of Metro-Goldwyn-Mayer films didn't frighten me; on the contrary, I wanted to see more of it. In fact, hadn't Metro-Goldwyn-Mayer produced the Tarzan movies with Johnny Weissmuller? We used to make a mad rush to see those films at the local cinema on Sunday mornings.

Tarzan reappeared in a Greek serial written by the journalist Nicos Routsos and published in inexpensive weeklies. But Routsos's Tarzan was a middle-aged man who jealously guarded his prerogatives, and he was much less likable than the Edgar Rice Burroughs character. The enormous success of this series was due to a new denizen of the jungle who was younger and stronger than Tarzan, with a darker complexion, and who had also been raised by a female monkey. In our eyes he had the incomparable advantage of being of Greek origin. His name was Gaour. The name has echoes of the Turkish word *giaour*, "infidel," a name the Ottomans used for the Greeks. In spite of his loyalty and kindness, Gaour annoyed Tarzan, and every now and then Tarzan would imagine ways to get rid of him and steal his fiancée, a hotheaded brunette from the Greek diaspora named Tatabou. I still remember a poignant scene in which Gaour and Tatabou were fashioning a Greek flag by coloring the four corners of a white piece of cloth blue so as to form a cross in its center.

These installments were abundantly illustrated. I was aroused by the powerful thighs and bomb-shaped breasts of the tiger-skin bikini clad Tatabou. Africa fascinated me all the more because I imagined it peopled with half-naked women. Several Greek pop songs in fact described the beauty of black women and heady tropical nights. Vassilis Tsitsanis expressed his desire to meet Tarzan in person in a humorous song:

> Should I ever win the lottery
> I'll go and see Tarzan
> And play for him my bouzouki
> To move him best I can.

When I was about fifteen, I discovered an Africa much less exciting than that of Edgar Rice Burroughs or Jules Verne, thanks to a novel by Mihalis Caragatsis entitled *Amri a mugu* and subtitled *In the Hands of God*. The author follows two wayward Greek sailors as they travel through the Dark Continent. They are searching for a mysterious character—a German, I seem to recall—whom they never manage to find. They earn a great deal of money, but little by little they lose their health and their minds because the local gods don't want them to succeed. I don't know if Caragatsis was familiar with Conrad's *Heart of Darkness*, which describes the quest of an almost mythical character lost in the jungle. I myself read this novel only much later, when I had already come to France. I remember people moving through dense shadows, and the cry shouted twice, like at the end of certain operas: "The horror! The horror!"

I'm almost sure that Caragatsis never names the language that provided him with the title of his tale. How does one say "God" in Sango? *Nzapa.* I just looked in the dictionary. One says *Nzapa.* I also just learned the expression *ngu ti Nzapa,* "the water of God," which designates rain. The preposition *ti,* "of," holds no more secrets for me. If there were a "god of the cold," he would certainly be called *Nzapa ti de. Ngu,* "water" is pronounced ngoo, and *de,* "the cold," is pronounced deh.

Were there many Greeks in Africa during the colonial era? I knew that one of my mother's cousins lived in Cape Town and that he worked for the railroads. My paternal grandmother, who was born in Alexandria in the late nineteenth century, never tired of boasting about the prosperity of the Greek communities in Egypt. She claimed to have known the poet Cavafy, which seemed quite extraordinary to me. She despised Nasser, who had caused the foreigners to flee Egypt. According to her, he was an ingrate.

"Without the Greeks," she used to say, "Alexandria would have forever remained a village."

She left Egypt in 1911, when she was pregnant with my father, in order to raise her son in the land of her ancestors. Her husband followed two years later, the time it took to sell his business and say goodbye to his sister Clotilde who was living in Bangui at the time. The only photograph I've seen of my grandfather was taken in Bangui, probably during this visit. He died in a typhus epidemic when he was very young, at the beginning of World War I.

"They're always talking about the epidemics ravaging Africa," my grandmother would say, "and yet it's Greece that killed my husband."

In the sepia photograph he is armed with a carbine, and his foot rests on the back of a cardboard lion. This décor seems to amuse him, for he has that hint of a smile that made him resemble my father so much. A few pots with exotic plants complete the picture, taken in the "Studio de Paris, rue Paul-Crampel, Bangui," as you can read in silver letters at the bottom. As a child I confused the man holding the rifle with my father, and I used to imagine I was the son of an adventurer. One day I learned this wasn't true. My father told me he had never been to Africa and that he was the director of a municipal funeral home.

"I attend to dead people," my father said defiantly. "Do you know what a dead person is?"

I did not. But I thought about the lion, whose head was resting on the ground and whose eyes were closed, and I answered "Yes."

I saw this picture for the last time when I closed up my parents' house in Athens, a house where no one lives any more. They both died, my mother nine years ago, and my father this year on March 7. The photo was in its usual spot, in a drawer of the buffet, carefully wrapped in tracing paper. I was struck once again by the resemblance between my father and my grandfather. I almost put the photograph in my pocket, but that didn't seem proper to me. The only thing I took with me was the letter my grandfather had written to his son right before leaving for the front. Did he have a premonition that his days were numbered? I don't know, but nonetheless he felt the need to express his affection for his little boy. My father didn't know how to read at the time. When he was old enough to decipher the letter, he was so moved by the first words that he had to stop reading at the third line.

He told me this story late last year, when his health was beginning to fail. He was eighty-six.

"When did you read his letter?"

"Never.... Not that I didn't try. But tears would always spring to my eyes immediately. I could never get beyond the third line."

Just thinking about that letter made him cry. I wiped his face with a Kleenex. In the box were pink, sky blue, and pale green ones.

"So who's going to read it?" I asked him, a little naively no doubt.

"You!" he exclaimed, sitting up. "You!"

Indeed I inherited that letter, but I still haven't taken it out of the envelope on which my father's name appears, written in ink in a slanted hand below which my own name is clumsily written in pencil. I'm in no hurry to read it. It can wait a bit longer to be read. It has already waited since 1911.

It was in the drawer with the photograph. I didn't touch anything else, I didn't throw out the medicine on the night table. One of the Kleenexes was half out of the box, as if it were about to take flight. All I did was put the top back on the Thermos where my father used to keep his cool water for the night. Then I left, closing the front door gently so as not to disturb the silence that would dwell forever after in the house.

Clotilde would regularly send us New Year's wishes on postcards that were also signed by her husband, André Bérémian, an Armenian from Marseilles. They were black and white pictures of buildings, fishing boats. I would plunge them into a bowl filled with water to get the stamps off. The words would come off as well, dissolving in the water, turning to ink once again.

The Latin adage that claims that writings remain seemed wrong to me. "No," I would think to myself, watching Coltilde's good tidings evaporate, "they do not remain."

Thanks to my great-aunt I had lots of stamps from French Equatorial Africa. My friends had none; I suppose there were few Greeks living in this region. There must have been more of them in Egypt, the Belgian Congo, the Union of South Africa, and Ethiopia, because it was relatively easy to collect stamps from those countries. King Farouk alone had a whole page in my album. I knew his profile by heart. My stamp collection confirmed in my mind the sizable Greek presence in Africa and taught me about the extent of Greek migration to the United States, Canada, and Australia; it showed me my compatriots' total lack of interest in Asia. Not one person I knew had Indian or Chinese stamps. Stamps from Eastern Europe were almost as rare. And yet many Greek Communists had sought refuge behind the Iron Curtain after the Civil War. Evidently they rarely gave word of themselves. Perhaps their letters were intercepted? Royalist Greece of the 1950s kept its distance from the Communist bloc, just as it kept its distance from Turkey, which had chased all the Greeks out of its territory. I had only three or four Turkish stamps.

Clotilde stayed in Athens for a short time in the mid-1960s and came to visit my parents. I recall a large, square-shouldered woman. There was a sense of vigor about her that was hardly compatible with her age and sex.

"Africa has made a man of Clotilde," my father remarked after his aunt had left.

She had thought I was younger than I was and had presented me with a teeny-weeny stool that stood on three crossed legs held together at the center. I tried it out anyway and found it to be extremely stable, which made me think that our seats had one too many legs. I didn't ask Clotilde a single question about Equatorial Africa; Tarzan no longer fascinated me. I now much preferred Dostoevsky's nefarious characters. My mother asked something about Clotilde's children, I think she had a girl and a boy. I left the room without waiting for the answer. I never did learn what André Bérémian was doing in Bangui.

I was in Athens on March 7. I learned of my father's death from his housekeeper, a Bulgarian woman who would watch television all day long while she knitted wool socks. It was raining that day. I wiped my feet very thoroughly before crossing the threshold of the house. I stroked my father's forehead. It was cold. Even after he was buried, I was still afraid of losing him, as if his death had been merely a warning, a bad omen. Ten times a day I would think of calling him to reassure myself.

I almost called him again when I got back to Paris, just as I had always done for the past twenty-eight years. I reached for the phone, but I didn't touch it. Then I set about unpacking my suitcase. As I was taking out my shirts, which had been carefully ironed by the Bulgarian lady, the telephone rang. I was squatting in front of the open suitcase on the floor. The sound frightened me. It rang only once, as if the person who was calling had realized he or she had dialed a wrong number, or as if he or she could not speak.

I hadn't anticipated that my father's death would be so painful. Hadn't I loved him enough? Did I think he hadn't loved me enough? Still, I had believed that his disappearance would affect me less than my mother's, that it would leave less of a void. In Paris I realized I'd been wrong. I thought about him so much that I tried to avoid making noise so as not to disturb him. I placed the dirty dishes very gently in the sink. I walked on tiptoe and had lowered the telephone's ring as much as possible, as if he were sleeping on the living room sofa.

Whenever anyone asked me how I was spending my time, I would invariably reply, "Right now I am attempting to make as little noise as possible." I wasn't writing. I went out only rarely and had very few visitors. From time to time I would approach my father, but I wouldn't speak to him. I would be satisfied to observe that he could still open his eyes, that he recognized me. I was nostalgic for his smile. His work had not made him somber or sad. He could recall a myriad of comical incidents that had occurred when someone had been placed in a coffin, during a burial, or during an exhumation. He would smile furtively, as if he were ashamed of his own cheerfulness.

Some nights I would miss the company of a woman, and yet I did nothing to fill this emptiness. I didn't call my ex-girlfriends, and I didn't make any attempt to meet new people. I simply called Alice to tell her my father had died. Little by little, the idea that I was too old to have amorous adventures occurred to me. The reflection my mirror sent back made me a little more anxious each day. I practiced dragging my leg behind me when I walked to see how it would feel. I was, in a way, preparing for the future.

Was it to take my mind off things that I began to think once again about that African language I had wanted to learn? The project I had come up with while I was in Greece seemed more exciting than ever. How would my father have reacted had he heard me reciting African words? He would have smiled, of course. Can one learn a language simply to amuse someone who is no longer here? I sometimes formulate questions that I don't attempt to answer. They are only stark question marks that shoot up like cacti from the desert of my mind. Another question preoccupied me even more: can you fall in love with a language the way you do with a woman? My first texts in French were written with a woman in mind. She had made me love certain words to distraction. Yet the African language of which I was dreaming was faceless. Sometimes I would give it the features of Gaour's companion, the sublime Tatabou. Other times, I would see it as an older woman—my father's housekeeper, for example. Yet I could see myself ushering it into my apartment. "Our inability to communicate will force us to remain silent for a long time.... She will be the first to speak. In the beginning I won't understand her.... And then I will. She must have some marvelous tales to tell." I still felt incapable of inventing stories that would have helped me through this difficult time.

The first person I told about my intention to study a new language was my friend Jean Fergusson, an ethnologist and journalist who was in charge of the travel section of *Le monde*. Jean had traveled widely. When he was young, he had lived among the Indians of the Amazonian Rain Forest. The Dalai Lama regularly sends him greetings. He's brought back so many artworks, everyday objects, and toys from his expeditions that his apartment on the rue de Buci resembles a second-hand shop. He has a map of the world where Australia, Africa, and South America are represented upside down and are at the top.

"There's no reason to believe that the North is on top and the South on the bottom like our cartographers do," he said. "By automatically placing Europe, Asia, and North America above the other continents, they suggest that the North's domination of the South is inscribed in the natural order of things."

The map in question was printed in Australia. I had the feeling I had taken a decisive step when I confided my project to him.

"If you were to learn the language of the Indians from Rio Purus, I would be in a position to help you."

"I'm interested in Africa," I replied, with a resolve I didn't know I had in me.

We were eating at the Trois Mousquétaires, a large brasserie on avenue du Maine where half the space is taken over by pool tables. Video clips played endlessly on a screen placed near the entrances. Customers had to shout at the top of their lungs to make themselves heard, as if someone hard of hearing were sitting at each table. I didn't see a single black person in the place. Jean has a weakness for this brasserie because of the pretty young waitresses with their dancer's tights. The name of the place no doubt reminds him of his mother, Lady Fergusson, who in the 1950s published a new and remarkable English translation of the saga of the Musketeers. She died when Jean was about ten, in a fire that destroyed the Fergusson castle in Yorkshire. His father disappeared for good after the tragedy. He was a Frenchman of Polish origin with an unpronounceable name. When Jean came of age, he decided to use his mother's name.

"Everyone is interested in Africa at one point or another in life, and no one knows why," he declared after much thought. "Conrad went there wondering what his expedition signified. Gide was in the same state of mind. Though neither of them ever had reason to regret his decision. Africa inspired Conrad to write a wonderful novel and Gide to write his first political texts. When he got back to France, Gide denounced the hard labor imposed on the indigenous people by the rubber companies. You're thinking of going there, too, I suppose?"

His question disconcerted me.

"No," I replied, hesitantly. "I simply want to learn a language."

He looked at me, perplexed, and seemed slightly upset. Then he confessed that during the course of his various stays in Africa he had only learned some of the basics of Swahili and Peul. I asked him to write down the names of a few languages. He wrote on the back of his business card. To Swahili and Peul he added Wolof, Bamana, Songhai, Mossi, Hausa, Yoruba, Ewe, and Igbo. With each word he wrote, my pleasure grew. "These are keys," I thought. "He is giving me an entire set of keys." I found each of these words held an undeniable charm, yet none of them in the end seemed superior to the others. Was the language I was going to study on this list? I had a feeling it wasn't. "When I hear its name, I'll recognize it immediately."

"I think the only person who can help you choose a language is Paul-Marie Bourquin," he concluded. "He knows several of them, he spent much of his life in Africa, and his wife Mathilde is a linguist. They're both retired now, they live in Beauvais. I'll be happy to go and see them with you one Sunday. I met them thirty years ago, on Mount Cameroon."

We parted in the corridor of the subway station at Gaîté without my having asked him a single question about his health. I was happy just to see that he looked so well. He's been undergoing chemotherapy for skin cancer over the past year. His doctor, Professor Préaud, thinks he's out of danger. Nevertheless I feel slightly apprehensive every time I say goodbye to my friend. I deplore this feeling; it's as though I attribute some evil power to it, yet I cannot manage to shake it.

We went to see the Bourquins two weeks later, on Sunday, May 9. It was a spring-like day, the highway was packed leaving Paris, and completely empty in the other direction. I now know how to say "car" in Sango: *kutukutu*. We took Jean's car (*kutukutu ti Jean*). He doesn't have much faith in mine (*kutu-kutu ti mbi*).

"All the Parisians have taken it into their heads to learn an African language and they're all going to seek advice from Paul-Marie," he said. "We'll find a really long line in front of his house when we get there."

He was overjoyed at the thought of seeing his friends again.

"If you only knew all we've been through together," he added nostalgically.

I was not nearly as happy as Jean. I imagined Paul-Marie as both a strict professor and an explorer hardened by a life in the outdoors, who would be disappointed as much by my ignorance of Africa as by my scrawniness. I was convinced that our meeting would take place in a room filled to bursting with terrifying masks. No matter how many times Jean told me our host was a courteous and affable gentleman, I couldn't help seeing the names of the towns we passed on our way—L'Isle-Adam, Ronquerolles, Sainte-Genevieve—as so many stations of the cross, at the end of which I would go through agonies.

The Bourquins live just outside of Beauvais, in a little hamlet of about ten houses. Theirs is hardly any different from any other, neither bigger nor newer. The man who came to open the gate of the property was tall, dressed in a roomy beige sweater. His hair was white, parted on the side, which gave him a youthful appearance. He must have been nearly eighty.

He took Jean in his arms and said, "So, Fergusson, you still remember your old pal?"

And then he put his hand out to me, fixing his blue eyes on me. What was he thinking about? Despite all the years I've spent in France, I still don't know how to read the expressions of blue-eyed people. The color disconcerts me. I used to find it cold. This is no longer the case. I am simply incapable of deciphering it. I handed him a copy of *The Tin Soldier*.

"We'll read this with great interest," he assured me.

His skin was as white as it would have been had he never left the Oise region. We walked through a vast area planted with relatively young trees before arriving at the terrace in front of the house, where a table had been set for lunch. Mathilde didn't get out of her armchair. She just smiled vaguely our way. Her sparse blond hair peeked out from a black headband.

"Welcome," she murmured.

Resting on her lap was a white cat wrapped in a blanket of the same color as her husband's sweater. With a look of someone who likes his food, Paul-Marie said he had prepared a rabbit with pearl onions for us. He brought Mathilde's meal to her on a tray. His gestures were rather nonchalant, yet he bustled about continually.

I was silent for almost the entire lunch. I didn't eat much either, as if frugality were the only attribute on which I could pride myself. Paul-Marie and Jean exchanged information about the fate of friends whom they hadn't seen for ages, referred to events that had occurred during their journeys. They praised the tea grown on Mount Cameroon. Paul-Marie watched his wife out of the corner of his eye; she was seated somewhat off to the side. She had difficulty swallowing her food, and she breathed noisily. Eating made her breathless.

Jean pulled a little bit of blackish cord folded in two from his pocket. It formed a ring at the fold thanks to a knot that joined the two halves. It bore a slight resemblance to a female figure. Paul-Marie examined the object, handling it very carefully. They didn't think it worthwhile to show it to me, but I noticed a few additional knots on each side of the main knot. Was it some kind of grigri or rosary?

"Colonel Peterson brought it back for me from Nigeria," Jean said.

"Have you heard from that dear man?" asked Mathilde.

I had been convinced she hadn't been following our conversation.

"He got married!"

"How about that! I thought he didn't like women."

Jean lamented the legal proceedings instituted by large pharmaceutical corporations to keep the poorer countries from cheaply producing the medicines they needed.

"The current price of AIDS treatment is completely out of reach for the eighty million Africans who are HIV positive. The corporations care more about the bottom line than they do about health."

"It's scandalous," I remarked.

After which I took a little sip of wine. My novel was poised on the edge of the table. "They won't read it. They'll stop on page twenty-two, when Martine begins to talk to the tin soldier." There were no tropical plants in the garden. Around the terrace, in well-tended flowerbeds, geraniums, hydrangeas, and petunias were planted. The Bourquins were in the process of forgetting Africa. From time to time I would peer out into the shadows forming beneath these clumps of flowers and under the trees. Was I expecting to see some preposterous animal appear? I saw only cats strolling about with the same lazy gait as their master. They would come into the house through a double glass door that led to the living room. I could make out a good part of this room, decorated with old plates and paintings in gilded frames. I wondered if the Bourquins had any children. "They had a baby boy who was kidnapped in the jungle by a female monkey."

Paul-Marie returned his wife's tray to the kitchen. Immediately the white cat jumped gracefully back to his spot on Mathilde's lap.

"I'm going to get my hammock from the car," said Jean.

"Do you still take your hammock with you everywhere?" I asked Jean mockingly.

"Yes! I got into the habit when I was in the Amazon!"

Paul-Marie moved his chair so as to face me directly.

"Fergusson tells me you want to learn an African language."

He was looking at his hands, which he had crossed on top of the table as he eased his plate back slightly. Was he waiting for an explanation from me? Should I confess to him that I myself was surprised by my intention? Would he accuse me of frivolity if I confided this to him? I looked skyward for some inspiration. The sun was shining down on the treetops.

"That's good."

His approval took a load off my mind; it spurred my imagination in an unexpected way. I saw myself conversing in the heart of the rain forest with a black man whose face was decorated with circumflexes. Why would he have disapproved of my curiosity about African languages when he had devoted his life to studying them? Perhaps he understood me better than I understood myself. But my enthusiasm quickly abated.

"There are hundreds of languages in Africa," he said in a quiet voice. "In Cameroon alone two hundred are spoken. Do you know any Arabic?"

I answered that I knew only a few words, such as *dunya*, "the world," which we use in Greek. One of Marcos Vamvakaris's songs goes

> The *dunya* is but an illusion,
> Just like life.

"I'm asking you this because some of the most widespread languages—Swahili, Hausa, Peul—have borrowed freely from Arabic. We can eliminate them. We can also eliminate the ones that have not yet been studied scientifically. So many still remain. I don't see how I can help you make your choice."

I felt dizzy, as if I were sitting on the highest branch of a baobab tree. Did he notice my disappointment? His expression became cheerful, mischievous.

"Do you know why the Arabs never managed to conquer central Africa? Because of the tsetse fly. The Arabs were stopped by flies! The flies killed their horses!"

I thought our interview was over, for he threw his head back and closed his eyes. Mathilde was dozing in her armchair, one hand resting on the cat's back. As for Jean, he had disappeared into his hammock, suspended from two pine trees. Paul-Marie's face became expressionless in sleep. "I didn't come all this way to watch you sleep!" Why had he avoided talking to me about the languages he knew? Was he afraid I would turn up in Beauvais every Sunday? Did I need to shout Tarzan's cry of the jungle to wake him? Just then Mathilde's cat had the good sense to jump on the table and place a paw on the edge of Paul-Marie's plate. The old man at last opened his eyes.

"What are you doing here, you?" he said to the cat.

Then he got up, motioning me to follow.

"I'll try to find you something in my library."

He led me into a vast room lined wall to wall with books. It had probably been an old barn; its roof could be seen through the framework. Several ladders positioned about the place provided access to the highest shelves.

"Are all these books about Africa?"

"Yes."

I had had no idea of the extent of my ignorance, its true proportions. Had I thought I was familiar with just one of the many books that surrounded me, I would have breathed a bit easier. But I didn't dare ask him if Edgar Rice Burroughs's book was among those in his collection. Paul-Marie had climbed up one of the ladders and was examining a row of volumes.

"Most of the language textbooks were written by missionaries whose knowledge of their subject was less than perfect."

Still more books were piled on the windowsills, on the desk, and on a stool. I noticed a statue of a naked black man on the computer table. The figure looked as if he were spitting: a thin rod extended from his mouth in a downward arc. His right hand was cupped to his ear as if to help him hear better. "He's not spitting," I thought, "he's speaking. The rod represents his words. He's asking a question and he's eager to hear the answer." Paul-Marie climbed down from the ladder. He had trouble squatting to check the works on the lowest shelf, and he rubbed his lower back. My father used to make that same gesture. Suddenly I thought about the photograph of my grandfather taken in the Studio de Paris in Bangui.

"What language do they speak in Bangui?"

"Sango."

At first I didn't realize that he had just uttered the name of the language I had been called upon to adopt. "I'm learning Sango": I thought up this sentence out of sheer curiosity, to test the sound of it. Still, I found it rather nice.

"Sango," he repeated, putting away the book. "I have a Sango textbook that's pretty good. Would you like to learn Sango?"

"My grandfather's sister spent almost her entire life in Bangui."

"Yes, there were a lot of Greeks there at one time. One of the main food shops in the city belonged to a man named Dimitris.

His name wound up being given to the corner where the shop was located. It became 'Dimitris's corner.'"

"Clotilde probably did her shopping at Dimitris's.... She must have known a few words of Sango. Perhaps the Studio de Paris is still open on the rue Paul-Crampel." I wanted to help Paul-Marie get up, but he preferred to lean on the bookshelf.

"Sango is the vehicular language of the Central African Republic, which used to be known as the Oubangui-Chari. At first it was spoken only by the Oubangui boatmen. There are several other languages in the country—Gbaya-Manza, Banda, Nzakara, for example—but only Sango is understood by just about everyone."

Shouldn't I be setting my sights on a more marginal language, Nzakara for example? "He'll tell me there are no books on Nzakara, there is only one article that appeared in 1928 in the poetry review *The Hermit's Well*." Nonetheless, I tried out the sentence "I'm learning Nzakara." It didn't seem very convincing to me. "I never knew how to speak Nzakara" sounded much more fitting.

"It's the language of power, I presume," I said, jokingly.

"You're quite mistaken."

He was now searching through the other side of his bookshelves.

"The spread of Sango was carried out by tradesmen and missionaries who had to go down the river to penetrate the heart of the country. In spite of its popularity, and even though it is the surest link among the country's various ethnic groups, it is not taught in the schools. Only French is taught, just as under colonial rule. Sango is treated like a subaltern, vulgar language by the authorities."

Modern Greek was long called vulgar. Greeks were not allowed to use the language they spoke—known as Demotic

21

(from *demos*, the people)—at school or in their dealings with the administration. The Greek government had set up a scholarly language—Katharevousa (from *katharos*, pure)—as the official language. It was supposed to prove the unfailing continuity of Hellenism through the centuries. "Sango is the Demotic of the Central African Republic," I thought. The light outside was fading rapidly. What if Paul-Marie couldn't locate the textbook he was looking for? I turned toward the statuette that possibly represented some divinity, and I prayed to it to make him find it.

"Here we are!" cried Paul-Marie.

He was holding two books in his hands, a small one with a blue cover and a much bigger one with a yellow cover. He started to hand them to me but stopped in the middle of his gesture.

"Do you really want to learn Sango?"

"I do."

I uttered these words as clearly as if it had been a wedding ceremony. "I shall learn the language of the Oubangui boatmen." The blue book was the textbook mentioned. It was signed by a Professor W. J. Reed, of the University of Toronto, and dated from 1970. The second work was a Sango-French dictionary. Beneath the author's name, one Marcel Alingbindo, I was surprised to see Mathilde's: "with the collaboration of Mathilde Bourquin," it read. It had been published in 1978 under the auspices of the Society of Linguistic and Anthropological Studies of France.

"Your wife knows Sango?"

"She studied it some thirty years ago.... You can keep these books, I'm sure Mathilde has other copies."

He told his wife with a satisfied air that I had chosen Sango. She became more animated, propping herself up in her armchair.

"I've almost forgotten it completely," she said. "And yet I used to speak it fluently. Are there some languages that are forgotten more easily than others? I mostly remember the mistakes I made in the beginning."

Jean was at the far end of the terrace with his hammock carefully folded under his arm and his eyes fixed on his car. I recalled that he had a date at 9:30 with a young Italian woman.

"Sango is a tonal language," Mathilde warned me. "The pitch of the voice often varies from one syllable to the next. There are normally three registers: low, middle, and high."

I was getting my first lesson in Sango. Jean came up to us, he was becoming impatient.

"Sometimes the pitch determines the meaning of words. *Kua* said in a deep voice means 'work,' and said in a high-pitched voice it means 'death.'"

"The same word is used to mean both work and death!" said Jean with amazement.

"I'm trying to explain to you that it is not the same word!"

Paul-Marie promised he'd look for the address of Marcel Alingbindo, the author of the dictionary.

"He works for the CNRS, but he doesn't live in Paris any more. Whenever you have questions for Mathilde, come and see us."

He walked us to the gate, the white cat right behind him. Before I climbed into the car, I stroked the animal's head to thank it for its kind intervention on my behalf.

Jean was rather irritated. Had I taken advantage of him? Was he afraid of missing his date with the Italian woman? It was only 6:30, and light was still falling on the countryside.

"Are you really going to read those?" he asked, indicating the two books with his chin.

"I'm going to try."

"Why did you choose Sango?"

"It's hard to explain why one chooses a language when one has no reason to learn it."

What was on the stamps from French Equatorial Africa that were in my collection? Landscapes? Animals? A hippopotamus performing its ablutions in the Oubangui? We had been quiet for a long time. Where had all the cars that had been on the road in the morning gone? Very few were headed into Paris. When we reached the exit for Noailles, I asked Jean if the cord with the knots in it had any magical properties.

"It protects you from illness. The knots form obstacles to the illness's evolution."

He talked to me about Sandra, whom he had met at the hospital when she was visiting her mother.

"One evening Sandra sang a lullaby. I heard her through the partition. Her voice made such an impression on me that I went out in the hall with my intravenous drip and waited for her to appear. I waited quite some time, despite the night nurse's admonitions."

I imagined Jean in his gray pajamas, leaning on his intravenous drip like a tired sentry on his spear.

"She's only twenty-seven. She sings in the choir of the Opéra de Paris. She was born in Pesaro, like Rossini!"

Why hadn't the idea of learning Italian—such a musical language—even crossed my mind?

"We'll go see her at the Opéra if you'd like. Unfortunately, because she's so tall, they put her in the last row of the choir. It's too bad, because she's magnificent."

Jean has a tendency to attribute to his new conquests more good qualities than they actually possess. His gaze magnifies their beauty. His intelligence adds wit to their words. His need to love is so great that all women seem lovable to him. The disappointments he has experienced haven't left their mark on him. He forgets them, I think. I, on the other hand, remember each and every one of my disappointments very clearly. They have made me mistrustful, skeptical. Unlike Jean, who easily ascribes imaginary good qualities to women, I am more inclined to take away the ones they actually possess. He is probably more generous than I. He told me that he had gone to lunch with Sandra twice.

"Tonight she's coming to my place. We're eating in."

Although I would certainly have been content to spend the evening with a beautiful, twenty-seven year old Italian woman who could sing me a lullaby, I was not for all that unhappy with my fate. I too was eager to go home, to browse through my new books in peace. I was sure that Sango wouldn't disappoint me.

"I feel like my apartment makes me seem older," he confided. "I can detect a look of astonishment in the eyes of the young women who come to my place and see my collections for the first time. I'm sure they wonder how old I am."

We were driving through the gloomy Parisian suburbs. A man appeared briefly at a window and glanced rapidly toward the street. "He wanted to make sure that nothing was happening."

"Do you still see Alice?"

"Very rarely. I don't tell her my secrets and she doesn't tell me hers. We've stopped being lovers without managing to become friends."

"You'll have to find a replacement for her. How old are you?"

He knows I'm three years younger than he is, yet he still asks me my age from time to time. I wasn't so sure I needed a replacement for Alice.

When I walked into my apartment, I was overcome with a sense of anguish. The stillness of the objects seemed suspicious to me. I imagined that it must have replaced a lively agitation, and that all my pieces of furniture had moved back into their usual spots when they had heard my footsteps on the landing. I went toward the sofa and touched its back hesitantly. It didn't respond. Was it sleeping? It surely slept more soundly than the other pieces of furniture. I left my books on the desk.

I realized it was too late at night to begin studying a language. Still, I was curious to take a look at the map of Africa in the *Larousse*. I have an old, 1948 edition of the encyclopedia. The Africa inside was still dominated by European powers. The French colonies, which represented about a fourth of the continent, were a pretty pink color. For the British possessions, the map's creator had selected a lemony yellow. I had to use a magnifying glass to locate the city of Bangui. It's on the right bank of the Oubangui; the left bank belongs to the Belgian Congo. The Chari is a river that goes through the north of the country. I discovered that French Equatorial Africa was composed of the Oubangui-Chari, Chad, and Cameroon.

I looked at the dot that represented Bangui for a long time, as if I were expecting to see a real city gradually come into view. Maybe one day I would have the desire to meet a boatman in a pirogue.

2

Speaking French was always more difficult for me than writing it. Alveolopalatal fricatives and unvoiced vowels disconcerted me. I could not understand how the joining of the "o" and the "e" in *coeur*, for example, could lead to such a thin, reedy sound. Compared to Greek, which is a rather resonant language, French seemed almost silent to me. I had the impression that French people spoke without opening their mouths.

Sango has no alveolopalatal fricatives. The "e" resonates almost as clearly as it does in the word *bec*, like "deck" in English. "U" is pronounced "oo." The letter "g," "ga," is always hard, starting in the back of the throat, like in "gangrene." Bangui should thus be written Bangi and not Bangui, as it is in French. In Sango, Bangui is pronounced Bangwi. I really want to adopt the rules of written Sango for proper names from now on. I shall write Bangi when I want to talk about the capital, and Ubangi when I need to talk about its river. The city of Bangassou that I located in the east of the country, with the help of my magnifying glass, should be spelled Bangasu, considering that in Sango the "s" is unvoiced even if it falls between two vowels.

I sometimes read Sango words aloud, at the risk of disturbing the peace of my neighbors. Perhaps they think illegal immigrants have besieged my apartment? Sango is a sonorous language, probably closer to Greek than to French; it encourages the voice to use its entire range. It seems as if it were conceived in a tumultuous environment, in the heart of a huge marketplace or during a night of celebration. No doubt the people who lived along the river needed such a language to speak to each other across it. Central Africans radically transformed the French words they adopted: *jusque* has become *zusuka, encore, angoro, docteur, dokotoro, chef, sefu*. France is called *Faranzi* and Greece, *kodoro ti mbi*, let's not forget, *Geresi*. As for the Central African Republic, its name in Sango is much more appealing: it is called *Beafrika*, that is, "Heart-of-Africa."

Sango has a few disquieting consonants that have no equivalent either in French or in Greek. They are transcribed with two or three letters but have to be pronounced in a single utterance. What then is the single sound that corresponds to *mv, kp, gb, ngb*? I need so much time to try to blend these letters together and to avoid stressing each one of them individually that I forget to breathe. I don't know if the coughing fits I occasionally experience are caused by tobacco or by words like *kpengba*, which means, appropriately, "hard," "difficult."

The first syllable of *kpengba* is high-pitched, the second low-pitched. According to Marcel Alingbindo's textbook, which uses the acute accent to indicate the high pitch and the grave accent for the low one, I should really write *kpéngbà*. Non-accented syllables belong to the middle register. For now I have to make do with writing the way the Catholic and Protestant missionaries who translated the New Testament did, without any accents at all. They deliberately disregarded the different tones: "We don't need tones to make ourselves understood," they affirm. It is possible. Apparently they are pronounced much less distinctly today than in the time of the Ubangi pirogue boatmen. In gaining a broader audience, Sango lost much of its flavor. The Gbayas, who are one of the largest ethnic groups in the country, speak a Sango that uses two tones, for the simple reason that their own language has just two. Linguists deplore this change, not only because there are many words, like *kua*, whose meaning can only be made clear by the modulations of the voice, but also, and especially, because they believe that the suppression of its distinctive characteristics will harm the language's memory. I cannot but agree with them. If the Greek language managed to hold on to its identity, it's because it remembers having been, once upon a time, the language of a blind poet.

Sometimes I try to sing some of the sentences cited in the textbook or in the dictionary. Alas, I have even less talent for singing than I do for languages. When I attempt to learn the tones I'll probably need a teacher. Shall I go back and see Mathilde? Her husband still hasn't sent me Marcel Alingbindo's address. Clumsy as my efforts are, they nonetheless make the language hop and skip. With every word, or almost, Sango begins a little dance, as if it were trying to recall a tune it had heard long ago.

I try to play my two roles — professor and student — to the best of my abilities. As soon as I learn a word, I hasten to teach it to myself:

"Do you know how to say 'tomorrow' in Sango?"

"How?"

When I was in school I never asked my teachers questions. I was bored in class. Just the sight of the blackboard was enough to depress me.

"How?" I ask again.

I make myself wait for my answer in order to pique my curiosity.

"*Kekereke!*" I declare at long last.

"Why, it's an onomatopoeia!"

"Precisely. You will notice that one says *cocorico* in French and *koukourikou* in Greek. Is this because the rooster's cry varies slightly from one country to the next? Well, it doesn't matter. In Sango, this onomatopoeia was used to form a noun that means 'tomorrow.'"

Sometimes the affected manner I take on in my role as teacher makes me want to laugh.

"And how do you say 'today'?" I ask slyly.

"We'll look at that later."

"*Kekereke?*" I suggest.

"*Kekereke.*"

How many words have I retained in six weeks of work? Not many. I learned more quickly when I was younger. My mind is slow to cross the distance that separates words. It lingers on the blank spaces as if they too were part of the language. Will I have the strength to make it to the end of the task I have set for myself? I realized just how huge it was as I was leafing through W. J. Reed's textbook. Had I underestimated Sango, as one does so easily when one doesn't know a language? But it would be even more painful to go backwards and forget the little I've learned. This is because one becomes attached to words, like one does to people and things. I was sensitive to the quaint charm of the metaphor *ngu ti Nzapa*, "the water of God." In ancient Greek there was an equivalent: Zeus is raining, they said. I imagine that my father, who was very devout, would have appreciated this metaphor, and that he would have been happy to depart on a rainy day. I hadn't expected to find a term as biting as *de* in the vocabulary of a tropical country. It renders perfectly the sensation I had when I touched my father's forehead. He passed away on March 7: browsing through the short chapter that W. J. Reed devotes to numbers, it was fated that I should stop on that number. It has a seriousness, a weight in Sango that neither Greek nor French gives it: *mbasambara*, that's how you say "seven" in Sango. On the other hand, the two high notes that go with *kua*, "death" (I should really write *kúá*), make me feel uncomfortable. They ring false in my ears, they mock the word, they lack respect for its meaning. *Kekereke* delighted me, and so did *kutukutu*. The noun that I prefer, however, is the one given to fickle women and prostitutes. They are called "butterflies," which in itself is rather common, but the word for them is delicious: *pupulenge*. Marcel Alingbindo says it is an insult. I never tire of savoring it.

Not only do the words I have already studied encourage me to keep going, so do those I don't know yet. The objects surrounding me are a constant reminder that I still don't know their names in Sango. How do you say "pencil," "paper"? How do you say "eraser" or "ashtray"? I find myself in the middle of unknown words that are constantly calling out to me. Sango has brought me back to the time when I first arrived in France. I was very attentive to smells then, I would sniff the air like a dog. What was the first French word that really seduced me? *Promiscuité*, "promiscuity," I believe. I'm sure, in any case, that I loved that word. How do you say "to get up"? I ask myself this question each time I prepare to interrupt my work. My ignorance makes me clumsy. Am I supposed to lean an elbow on the table before I push my chair back from it? I'll need to learn some verbs as quickly as possible.

I notice that everything has two names for me, one Greek, the other French. Why is it that it took me so long to become aware of this? I also realize that I don't see objects in exactly the same light when I name them in one language or in the other. In French, the word for hammer, *marteau*, reminds me of the bed I built myself to save money when I first arrived in Paris. In Greek, the same term — *sphyri* — makes me think of my father, who loved to tinker. He took great care of his tools, he would clean them with a cloth soaked in paraffin oil. One day I came upon him as he was nailing shut a coffin in a municipal warehouse.

"Is there somebody in there?" I had asked.

There was. My father was vigorously hitting the nails, driving them in deep, as if he thought the dead man capable of escaping.

The word "onion" in French (*oignon*) also appears in a different light in both languages. Its Greek version (*crommydi*) takes me back to my mother, whom I would often see browning onions in a frying pan, whereas its French label conjures up the kindly features of the woman who runs the fruit and vegetable stand on the rue de Lourmel where I shop.

The memories I associate with Greek are much older than those the French language calls up. My mother tongue knows how old I am. French makes me twenty-four years younger. That's quite a bit. I always feel that my French texts are lighter than my Greek writings.

I'm starting to think that learning a language is like taking a dip in the fountain of youth. Sango doesn't remind me of anything, my memories are alien to it, and it gives me the agreeable illusion that I can start anew. It invites me to play, like French used to. It is less painful for me to talk about my father's death in Sango than in Greek. I now know how to say "my father is dead." This, in fact, is the example used in the dictionary to illustrate the verb *kui*, to die: *Baba ti mbi a kui*. The lone "a" doesn't indicate the past tense, as it does in French. It doubles the subject whenever it is not a personal pronoun. *Baba ti mbi a kui*: I write this calmly. I forget to be moved.

Georges, my publisher, is only six years older than I, yet he seems much, much older to me. This is probably because his knowledge is so vast that it allows him to talk about authors from the past as if he had rubbed shoulders with them. He is a remarkable raconteur, with a good feel for detail and a good nose for suspense. He has already had me accompany him to a séance led by Alexandre Dumas, a birthday party at the Brontë sisters' home, a night of drinking in St. Petersburg with Dostoevsky and the Abbot of Saint Savior's Monastery. I suspect that he invents all the stories he tells as he goes along, or that, at the very least, he alters them to suit his needs of the moment, for he has never published a thing. I have a hard time believing that anyone can entirely do without the pleasure of making things up. Moreover, he has interesting opinions on all kinds of subjects, particularly on the novel, which according to him was born in the great nineteenth-century railway stations. He claims that railway travelers are questions that only the novel can answer. A few years ago when he came to Athens he saw the unassuming building that is its station.

"This is why the Greek novel has trouble asserting itself! You don't have a real train station yet!"

33

"But we have a port," I objected.

Does he avoid revealing his literary tastes out of modesty? I don't even know what he thinks of my books. Only on one or two occasions could I really tell that he had in fact read them. He prefers sarcasm to praise. He is extremely critical; perhaps this is what keeps him from writing.

He doesn't like to broach certain matters. We never discuss either my private life or his. He isn't married and doesn't have children. What does he do when he leaves work? He must spend his nights reading; I don't see how else he could be knowledge-able about so many things. Only two framed photos adorn his office, one of Jules Verne in front of his yacht, the *Saint-Michel*, and the other of Al Capone in a bathrobe, seated with a fishing reel at the stern of a whaling boat. Both Verne and Capone are wearing the same relaxed, amused expression.

I went to see him one morning last week. I was somewhat apprehensive because I was afraid that he would ask me about the novel I was supposed to turn in at the end of the year, and I had not, of course, even begun it. For a year and a half already he has been paying me advances for this novel. "I have at least to be in a position to tell him the subject of the book," I thought as I was walking down the stairs to the subway. I tried to come up with something during the ride, but, alas, between my station and the Sèvres-Babylone station, where Georges's publishing house is, there are only five stops. I arrived empty-headed at his office door. "I'll tell him that I haven't yet recovered from my father's death." Just as I was getting ready to knock, I heard a cry from within. It wasn't my publisher's voice.

"I answered 'Here!' when you needed me! I always answer 'Here!' when my friends need me! I spent a whole night hanging around in the cold in Vitry-le-François! It was fifteen degrees out! Don't you remember? In the middle of winter!"

"I paid you for that," Georges answered calmly.

"Oh, yes, you paid me, but I still need money! I have six children!"

"Six? Are you sure?"

The other man said nothing.

"No, not really," he admitted, noticeably lowering his voice. "Five, maybe? What's the difference? I don't see them any more. They've all run away, they avoid me! They don't want to help me either!"

As if I were an actor in a play, I knew that the time had come for me to make my entrance on stage. So I opened the door.

"How's it going?" I inquired enthusiastically.

My publisher greeted my arrival with relief. His visitor, a small, balding fellow in his sixties with bushy eyebrows was standing in front of his desk. At first he looked at me with hostility. He was wearing a torn, wrinkled, unimaginably dirty raincoat. It looked like a doormat for a barracks. His shoes were very expensive, made of light brown leather, but they were too big for him and had no laces. He recognized me.

"Why it's Mr. Nicolaides!"

He opened his arms as if to hug me. The notebook that had been wedged beneath his armpit fell to the floor.

"Why, it's Mr. Nicolaides! The famous author of *Dr. Remlinger's Conversion* and *Letter to Marika*!"

He picked up his notebook, blew on it, wiped it on his coat.

"Okay, okay, I'll give you a thousand francs and you'll leave us alone, all right?" said Georges.

"Do you know why he's paying me? Because I let him copy from me when we were in school! We did all our schooling together! I was a better student than he was! I had lots of talents, you know? I lost them all. . . I lost them all, just like that, pfuitt, they flew away!"

He pocketed the two 500-franc bills and slipped out.

I sat down in an armchair. Georges was tired. His face was reflected in the glass top on his desk. He looked like a playing card. There was nothing on the desk other than an ashtray and a small blank envelope. He likes to give people the impression that he doesn't work much and he makes files vanish as soon as he has looked at them.

"You've just met Jackie Santini," he told me, without abandoning his sullenness. "He had his moment of glory in the seventies, thanks to a diatribe against love pompously entitled *A History of Amorous Passion*. His was an original mind that became superficial over the years. A strange evolution, don't you think? He has ideas, but who doesn't?"

"How does he earn his living?"

I was intrigued by another question that I couldn't ask him: what on earth was Jackie Santini doing in Vitry-le-François on a winter's night?

"He sells his ideas to publishers and to writers like you. I have to say, he comes up with some pretty good titles."

He lit one of the three cigarillos that were sticking out of his breast pocket. He would smoke one in the morning, one after lunch, and one on leaving his office. I was smoking my pipe, so two clouds formed between us. "How do you say 'smoke' in Sango?" I hadn't thought once about the language of the Central African Republic since I had left home. I had the sense that the question hadn't come from me but from the language itself, that it had found a way to make me remember it. It reminded me of those jealous women who call their lovers on the phone every hour.

"Were you very close to your father?"

I remembered the fax he had sent me in Athens the day after my father died: he had drawn a cypress tree in the rain. Unusually for him, he had signed just his first name.

"We became closer after my mother died. We would console each other. Sometimes I'm still surprised that he's no longer here to take my mind off the fact that he's gone."

"He won't ask me anything about my work.... He'll wait for a better opportunity to question me, over lunch for example." This realization helped me relax and even made me want to talk to him more frankly than I had originally intended.

"Writing a book about my father doesn't tempt me for the moment. It would inevitably be a farewell book, like the one I wrote for my mother. Words would only confirm our separation. I still need to talk to him."

I looked at the envelope on the desk. Another envelope came to mind, bearing the names of two addressees, my father's and my own, and containing a very old letter.

"There is just one little story I would like to tell."

I spoke to him about the letter my father had given to me and of which he had only ever read the first three lines.

"I suppose you haven't read it either?" he asked me with a kind of anxiety.

"No. If my father were still alive, it would probably be easier for me to read it."

"I'm sure.... You would be less affected by it. But right now you are very affected by it, since your father gave it to you."

"But he didn't write it!"

Georges shrugged. He put the envelope in a drawer, as if he reckoned it had done its job.

"It lives on as the letter of a deceased father," he concluded.

I didn't mention anything about my interest in Sango to

him, yet I did tell him that I was reading, in my free time, a textbook I had come across by chance.

"It's the language of the Central African Republic," I added, thinking it might be useful to say so.

He knew. I had forgotten that he knew everything: he remembered that André Gide and his traveling companion, the filmmaker Marc Allégret, had learned a few words of Sango during their stay in Africa.

"It seems that Gide undertook the journey without knowing what he expected to get out of it.

"He had just finished writing *The Counterfeiters*. He had run out of ideas. He must have wanted a change of scenery. Unfortunately his travel diary, called *Voyage au Congo* even though he barely mentions the Congo in it, is rather disappointing. He is inordinately interested in little flowers and insects. It's the diary of a butterfly hunter!"

He was getting back his usual vivaciousness.

"He describes rather nicely the stench of a large chunk of hippopotamus meat drying in the sun before it is eaten. He spent almost a year in Africa, so he had no choice but to take an interest in people as well. He wound up detecting another nauseating odor, the one given off by the companies France had contracted to exploit the colonies' resources."

"He could have been an excellent teacher," I thought. I taught him in turn the name given to loose women and butterflies in Sango.

"*Pupulenge*," he repeated like an echo. "*Pupulenge....* Why, how charming!"

I was moved, as if I had invented this word, or as if Sango were my language. I was eager to go home and continue my work. He opened his calendar and noted, on that day's page, the word in question. He wrote *poupoulingué*, the French way.

"Don't you think we should make a date to have lunch?" he asked, leafing through the following pages.

He wasn't free before he was to leave on vacation in mid-July. We fixed our lunch date for Monday, August 23.

When I was three or four, I would spend my days either with my father at the funeral home that was housed on the first floor of the city hall, or with my mother. She worked in a very famous dressmaker's shop where costumes for the theater were also made. I preferred her shop, where there were only women who took very good care of me. They would sit me on their knees and gladly play with me; some of them had very opulent bosoms. The space had a glass roof and was as bright and warm as a greenhouse. The seamstresses worked in gray smocks. Even their legs were sweaty. I would get down on all fours to observe their legs while the muscles would contract and relax as they worked the pedals of the sewing machines.

"There's nothing to see under the machines," my mother would scold, while her colleagues laughed.

She wanted to get me away from my father's influence at all cost because, according to her, he only cared about having a good time with the widows who would come to his office. During her break, she would insist on making me read the signs hanging on the shop walls: "NO SMOKING," "EMERGENCY EXIT," "SILENCE IS GOLDEN." I could tell she had put a lot of hope in me, maybe all her hope, and this worried me sick because I had serious doubts about my abilities.

One of her colleagues, a tall, thin, blonde girl, had taken it upon herself to teach me arithmetic. She would look at me fixedly and speak to me deferentially, as if I belonged to a superior set. She didn't sit me on her lap, but I didn't mind because I didn't think she was very nice. She would line up several buttons on the sewing-machine table, then remove a few. I didn't understand why she did that. I was much more interested in the machine than in the buttons. I was dying to turn its wheel, which was fitted with a small wooden handle. These classes didn't last long. One morning the seamstresses found this girl, whose name I don't recall, hanging from one of the beams that supported the glass roof. She had hanged herself with the lace ribbons that were supposed to be used for making the costumes for Schiller's *Mary Stuart*. I was with my mother that morning. She wouldn't let me into the shop until the ambulance had left. I didn't ask any questions. I was merely content to take advantage of my teacher's absence to play with her machine. I managed to stick the needle into my index finger, right through the nail.

I would be slightly bored at the city hall. My father would give me crayons and paper, but I had no real gift for drawing either. I would stay in the office next to his. On his door, which he would close with care, there hung a braid of garlic. I would station myself near the window. Most often the bustle of the street was hidden by the hearses parked along the curb. From time to time, he would take me to the cemetery, where I was much happier. I would play ball with the priest's children and with the gravedigger Stanislas's son. We would use the two cypress trees planted three meters apart near the outer walls as the goal. Whenever I was alone, I would roll my ball among the graves, imagining I was up against the team of the dead. I would play all alone against the dead and I would win.

I wasn't scared of them. When I ran out of breath, I had no compunction about sitting down on the slabs of marble, which remained cool even in the middle of summer. I would look at the inscriptions carved on them. I wanted to learn to read without my mother's knowing it, to surprise her. One day, without making any particular effort, I managed to make out a name, that of Katerina G. Papageorgiou, deceased in 1951. I suddenly realized that the woman in question was someone I knew. I had seen her at home, since she had her dresses made by my mother. I was both sorry to learn of her death and delighted to decipher her name. Immediately I glanced at the inscription on the neighboring gravestone, and I managed to decipher it as well.

I waited until dinnertime to give my mother the good news. I asked her to show me her identification card, which I placed next to my plate. Then I began to read aloud all the information printed on it. My mother's maiden name was Mylona and her first name was Marika. Her hair was dark brown and her eyes were light brown.

"Where did you learn to read?" she asked, amazed, when I had finished.

"In the cemetery," I replied, as if it were the most natural thing in the world.

My father was much less relaxed at home than at the funeral parlor, where he would joke all day long with his old secretary, the mayor, the priest who officiated at the cemetery chapel, and with Stanislas, his acolyte. He had several faces in fact. As soon as a family in mourning entered the room, he took on a pained, almost indignant, expression, as if he had known the deceased and believed his loss to be profoundly unjust. He would recite the usual condolences with stirring conviction, stroke the children's heads, offer a liqueur to the widows. He always kept excellent liqueur in a lovely crystal flask with its thin neck and plump belly encircled by golden threads. He had got it from his mother, who had brought it back from Alexandria. I left it with Stanislas as a souvenir.

Did he really have affairs? It's not easy for me to accept. He spent a great deal of time in Church on Sunday. Long after mass had ended, he would remain kneeling there. What was he asking for in his prayers? Perhaps he wanted to be forgiven for the error of his ways during the previous week? Stanislas surely knows if he had mistresses. Would he agree to talk to me about it? And did I in fact want to know?

Every now and then my mother would explode in a fit of jealousy. Yet I'm convinced she wasn't in love with him. I suppose she felt humiliated. She suspected him of being ready to cheat on her with the first woman to come along, and yet she believed him incapable of becoming truly attached to the women he seduced. In other words, she reproached him not only for cheating on her, but also for cheating on the other women.

I think they could have had a more pleasant life together had my mother been less demanding and my father more available. She would constantly compare him to the ideal husband she had imagined in her youth, and she came up with so much criticism of him that it became discouraging.

"I would have loved to live with a brilliant man," she would say to me.

He wasn't brilliant. He wasn't even very cultured. He had a very particular sense of humor, but his jokes didn't make my mother laugh. To her they were merely evidence of a superficial mind. He didn't like to travel, whereas she would dream of long journeys. In spite of the fact that she was a working-class woman, she aspired to know the world's beauty. She made me go to the premiere of *Mary Stuart*. At the end of the play we went back to the dressing rooms, where she was congratulated for the costumes. The director held her hand for a long time. A few weeks later he called her at home. The day after my mother died, I found the program of that evening among her things, with a dried flower inside. She would complain of being lonely.

"If it weren't for you. . . ," she would say to me.

What would she have done if it weren't for me? Would she have left with the director? Would she have taken a job on an ocean liner?

I can't say there were a lot of fights at home. My parents saw each other rarely and spoke to each other even more rarely. My father would come home late. He would eat alone while my mother continued her sewing in the living room. I would do my homework on the same table. Through the kitchen door I could see my father, eating with his back to us. Once he had finished his meal, he would rinse his plate, kiss us on the forehead, and go up to bed by the narrow and rather steep wooden staircase to the second floor. My mother's nervousness would vanish immediately.

She would drop her work and ask me, "Would you like a cup of chamomile tea?"

We would chat.

My father only became attentive to her once she was hospitalized. During that whole long period he showed her unwavering affection. In the rare moments when my mother was able to think clearly she, too, would look at him with tenderness. I suppose they loved each other when they were young. And they loved each other again before separating forever.

Mama ti mbi a kui in 1990. A year later, I felt nostalgic for our past conversations, and I wrote her a long letter in which I gave her news of myself and my father. I needed to let her know how many good things were being said about her. I didn't intend to publish this text, but Georges insisted. He was right, as always. The *Letter to Marika* became my best-selling book. I think my mother, with her taste for travel, would have understood why I was interested in Sango. I would have been delighted to teach her how to say "I am all alone": *mbi yeke gi mbi oko*, which means literally "I am only me one." *Oko* is the number "one." I'm going to call Alice and tell her: "Don't you want to come over? I am only me one."

These days I am only me one every evening. Alice maintains that we shouldn't see each other any more because our story has ended. I'm always the one to call her. I'm having trouble breaking it off completely, as if she were a part of my family. The only people in Paris with whom I can talk about my parents are Alice and Jean. Alice met them one summer in Greece. My father fell a little in love with her at the time. He offered her an icon of the Annunciation that his friend Stanislas had painted and then called her every year to wish her happy birthday. Jean only met my mother when she had come to stay in Paris once. We had dinner in a Vietnamese restaurant on the rue des Carmes. I had just published my second novel. I gave my mother the very first copy I had received. She kissed the book's cover.

"It's such a shame that it's written in French!"

"I'll translate it into Greek," I promised her.

She remembered this dinner for the rest of her life. She said that she had never been so happy. She had adored the Vietnamese cuisine.

Once every two months Alice agrees to go out with me. I try to act jovial but come up against a wall. Her gaze is somber. She will never forgive me for the few affairs I had while we were together. We avoid speaking about the past. We don't share any projects for the future. We go to the movies or the opera, places that don't lend themselves to conversation. We always manage to find a way to argue during intermission. The singers I like she finds atrocious. She comes to life only when she is angry. She rejects the glass of champagne I offer her.

"Have you forgotten that I don't like champagne?"

I go to bed at a reasonable hour and wake up early. By seven at the latest I'm already deep in the dictionary. I promised myself I would read it from cover to cover. Did I mention that the book's size is impressive? Approximately six thousand words are listed in it. I'm not trying to learn them by heart. I'm content to read them carefully, along with the sentences that accompany them. I'm up to the letter "L."

At noon I fix myself a little lunch and then nap for an hour. I think I've been dreaming more since I've been living this monastic life. I suppose it stimulates my imagination. I start working again in the afternoon, after I've had a bath and made a few phone calls. Jean is going back in the hospital next week. I asked Mrs. Voula, one of my parents' neighbors in Athens, to water the trees in their yard. There are only four: two apricot trees, a lemon tree, and a mimosa. At eight I stretch out on the couch and absent-mindedly watch a little TV. Nothing holds my attention—not the news, not talk shows, not movies. I simply notice that Africa is hardly ever mentioned on the news. Once or twice I catch sight of a motionless lion staring at the horizon. He seems just as decrepit as I. "It's the Metro-Goldwyn-Mayer lion that got older," I think. I don't really mind that the programs aren't any good since I don't want to stay up late.

Whenever I go out to shop or do my laundry at the Laundromat on the rue de Lourmel, I experience an amazing feeling of freedom. I savor the sights on the street even though they aren't very exciting. I let myself be moved by the old men, by

45

the young girls smoking on the sidewalk in front of the beauty salon and the unemployment office, by the street sweepers and the young blue-eyed tramp begging in front of the wine-seller's stand. He leaves his post at 12:30 and returns at 2:00. Once I came upon him on another street as he was hurrying away. I was entirely open to giving him a coin, but it seemed tactless to do so when he wasn't asking anyone for anything. Is the black population growing in the neighborhood? Have I just become more sensitive to its presence? I see more and more Africans, especially at the Laundromat. The other day while I was drying my laundry, two big guys walked in carrying a ton of clothes. I advised them not to use machine number three, whose door didn't close properly, for which they thanked me warmly. They managed to stuff all their laundry into machine number four, packing it in as much as they could. Among my drying things was a pink scarf that had belonged to my mother and that I sometimes wear in winter. It was spinning around in the drum like a panic-stricken bird. From time to time it disappeared behind a white sheet, but it always returned to the foreground and, lighter and lighter, continued its circling. As I was leaving the Laundromat I greeted the Tunisian man who has the copy shop right next door. That day I came home with the feeling that I had had conversations.

There is no doubt that Africa now occupies a particular place in my mind. How else can I explain the fact that it took me so long to notice the elephant that is the symbol of the manufacturer of my refrigerator? I bought it six years ago, which is to say I had had plenty of time to notice the animal; it was clearly portrayed on the glass shelf that sat atop the vegetable bin. I'm sure I had already seen it dozens of times without really noticing it, without associating its image with anything else. And so I only really saw it about ten days ago. I thought for a brief moment I was hallucinating, that I was seeing an elephant where there was nothing. "I'll wind up seeing elephants everywhere." In Sango, the word for elephant is *doli*, and for elephants, *adoli*. Plurals are formed by adding the prefix *a-*. I practiced over and over forming the plurals of nouns I knew: *akodoro*, "countries"; *akutukutu*, "cars"; *adokotoro*, "doctors"; *apupulenge*, "girls."

Fifteen minutes after I began studying the dictionary again, I had been carried so far away that when the telephone rang, it upset me tremendously, just like when it rings in the middle of the night. I don't wonder who is calling, but rather if I'm there to answer the call. I know now that Sango is leading me somewhere, perhaps to a place where I will joyously notice my own absence. I avoid thinking about our destination. I content myself with following Sango's tracks, which is already difficult enough. It wanders over lands where almost all the plants and three quarters of the trees are unknown to me. Its syntax disconcerts me even more. It doesn't say anything the way I'm used to hearing it said. "I'm carrying a trunk on my head" becomes, "I'm carrying on my head trunk one." "There are three women in my bed" (an example I haven't found anywhere) most likely is said, "There are in my bed women three." I presume that the story of Snow White must be titled "Snow White and the Dwarves Seven"? I haven't forgotten that "seven" is translated as *mbasambara*.

Whereas in French, like in Greek, the negating adverb goes at the head of the sentence, in Sango it goes at the end. How can anyone not be surprised by a language that always presents things in a positive light, only to retract them immediately afterwards? If you want to express the idea that you no longer have parents, first you will say that you have them, and then you will add *pepe* (the first syllable is middle, the second deep, *pepè*), that is "not," "not at all," or, in Greek, *dèn*: "I have

47

my father and my mother not." "There are not three women in my bed" is said something like this: "There are in my bed women three not." Whenever two negative propositions follow one another, "I didn't know that you didn't come," W. J. Reed remarks, *pepe* will be repeated twice at the end. In other words, *pepe* is a kind of trap door in which the meaning of words is suddenly swallowed up. Greek and French express negation energetically, right off the bat. Sango, however, equivocates, takes the chance of expressing the opposite of what it means, cultivates suspense. The Sango sentence spins itself out beneath the shadow of a doubt.

An African who would have the curiosity to learn something about Greek would be just as confused as I am. "Why do you say that like that?" he'd constantly wonder. Sango sends me back the questions I ask it. Learning a foreign language forces you to ask questions about your own. I am thinking of both Greek and French here: I see them differently since I started moving away from them, distance brings them closer together and at times I have the illusion that they form a single language. Could I be using Sango in order to make peace with myself? Despite my countless voyages between my mother tongue and my adopted language, I always feel slightly troubled when I go from one to the other. They are definitely languages that know each other, that have spent time together, that have shared memories. I can make out their resemblance much better at present. Viewed from Bangi, the distance between Athens and Paris must seem totally insignificant.

"Why do your verbs have so many different forms? Why this need to make them agree with their subject? They seem like musical instruments that fall out of tune after each note. Why change their endings depending on the time their action occurs? Isn't it easier to indicate time by one appropriate word?

And why does the conjugation change so often from one verb to another? What's the point of so many rules and so many exceptions? And, finally, why are you so harsh with people who make mistakes when the language seems to have been conceived precisely so that mistakes should occur? No wonder people look so preoccupied in the street: they are practicing their conjugations because they're afraid of forgetting them." I'm sure that faces in Bangi are more joyful than they are in Paris or Athens. There are no conjugations in Sango. The Sango verb remains immutable. "I am" is translated as *mbi yeke*; "you are" is *mo yeke*; "he is," *lo* or *a yeke*. One still says *yeke* in the imperfect past and in the future as well. Yet the language makes a distinction among the immediate future, a relatively distant future, and a very distant future. They are announced by the adverbs *fade*—immediately; *ande*—later; and *gbanda*—much later. The recent past is designated by *ando*, and the past that is lost in the mists of time, by *giriri*. When the language wants to emphasize the finished nature of an action, it uses the verb "to finish," ending its proposition with *awe*, "it's finished." *Awe pepe*, "it's not finished," is used when an action is not yet completed. The notion of duration in the present is expressed with the auxiliary *yeke*, which in this instance takes on the same meaning as the phrase "to be in the process of." *Lo yeke kui* means "he is in the process of dying," "he is going to die." When it is by itself, the verb fluctuates between the present and the past. *Lo kui* is translated by "he is dead" rather than by "he is dying."

Why am I writing all this down? When I was learning French, I wrote down in a notebook everything I heard in the cafés, in the subway, even at the homes of people who invited me to dinner, like a reporter or a secretary. Writing allows you to make physical contact with language, to touch it. Perhaps I think that words are wild animals that need to be tamed? I'm trying to know them as much as I'm trying to have them get to know me.

What would someone who was content merely to read these pages retain of Sango? Would he or she remember that rain is called *ngu ti Nzapa*? That tomorrow is *kekereke*? That the "e" is an open "e": *kèkèrèkè, yèke, awè*? Would he or she have retained the fact that *giriri*, "formerly" and *gi*, "only," are pronounced "ghiriri" and "ghi," respectively? Would he or she be able to recite the pronouns *mbi*, "me," *mo*, "you," *lo* or *a*, "him"?

I don't claim to be writing my own Sango textbook. I just want to speak about this language the way one might speak about a woman. I suppose I must be starting to love it because I couldn't stand it if strangers showed too much interest in it. I would be terribly angry if I came across someone in a park deep in Marcel Alingbindo's dictionary or W. J. Reed's textbook. After much hesitation, I finally called the Institute of Eastern Languages, where several African languages are taught, to find out if Sango was one of them. I was almost relieved to learn that it isn't. I like to think I am the only Sango enthusiast in all of Paris, and even in all of France, and that it is only studied at a small college in Pennsylvania, at 10:00 PM on Tuesday evenings.

I'd like to take Sango lessons but not in a class. I also called the Embassy of the Central African Republic. The man who answered the phone didn't know any teachers of Sango and had never heard of Marcel Alingbindo. He had a deep voice. "He is the first Central African with whom I've ever spoken," I thought. I was tempted to say a few words in Sango to him. Would he have understood me if I had declared, *"Kodoro ti mbi Geresi"*? He seemed in a hurry to hang up. I didn't push the matter.

50

3

Will I wind up being as interested in the country as I am in its language? The fact is I wanted to get a better look at it than what I could gather from the *Larousse Encyclopedia*, so I went out one morning to find a more detailed, more recent map. The rain that was falling didn't dampen my enthusiasm.

I went to several travel bookstores without finding any map of or guide to the Central African Republic whatsoever. Some salespeople even had trouble identifying it and asked me if that was really its name. Only one old bookseller understood that Central African Republic referred to what used to be called the Ubangi-Chari.

"Oh, Ubangi-Chari," he sighed, as if recalling happy times. "They should have kept that name after independence, don't you think?"

"The country's real name is Beafrika. *Be* means 'heart' in the national language."

He had that same distracted gaze as my father. There was

so little color left in his eyes that it was impossible to make out what he was looking at. He saw me from far away.

It wasn't until around noon that I found what I was looking for near the Champs-Elysées, at the National Geographical Institute's store. I was so happy to have finally got my hands on a map that I almost bought two. The cashier was a big black man with gray hair wearing a striped shirt and a blue tie with elephants on it. Oddly, the animals were aligned vertically and looked as if they were falling.

The area of the Central African Republic is as great as that of France and Belgium combined. The map itself is so big that I had to unfold it on the carpet. I've left it there ever since. Each time I cross the room I look at it as if I were flying over the country in an airplane. Sometimes I like to examine it closely, so I sit on the floor. The entire country is green except for a minuscule desert to the north. How could it be otherwise? So many rivers crisscross it that it must be better to own a pirogue than a car there. The network of roads is not nearly as dense. The center of the territory is a pale green, and the south, a dark green. According to the key, pale green corresponds to the savanna. Now there's a word that means absolutely nothing to me. Where on earth would I have seen a savanna? Central Africa's savanna is rather flat. There are a few hills, symbolized by some kind of gray clouds, but no real mountains. There is nothing, in other words, that brings to my mind the bare mountains that tower above the parched landscapes of my beloved country. At sunset, to relax after a tiring day, Greeks turn their gaze to the sea. On what does the gaze of Central Africans come to rest? The sea is really far away. The Ubangi doesn't flow into the ocean, but into the Congo River. Perhaps they look at the Ubangi? They borrowed the word "sea" from the French *mer*. They say *lamere* (*lamèrè* according to the dictionary's accent system). They do have their own word for "island," however, *zua*. I suppose islands can be seen in the Ubangi, or in the middle of lakes, for there are lakes as well. I located two to the north of Bangi, Crocodile Lake and Sorcerers' Lake. I pictured myself in a small pick-up truck at the crossroads of the paths that lead to these two sites.

"Should I turn left or right, boss?" asked the driver, a big black man wearing a tie with tiny elephants on it.

"Right," I replied.

That's the way to Sorcerers' Lake.

The dark green represents vast forests. I hold my breath, the better to hear the dead branches crackling beneath the heavy footsteps of wildcats. Tarzan often held his breath. Are there wildcats in these forests? The largest of them begins to the west of Bangi and occupies the entire area up to the border with Cameroon. There are very few villages, and roads are almost nonexistent. I don't see why lions and panthers would shun this peaceful area through which a tributary of the Ubangi, the Lobaye, flows.

I felt an intense excitement as I gazed at the map of the capital, inset in a corner of the larger map. Bangi is shaped like a fan whose branches are represented by Barthélemy-Boganda Avenue, the avenue de France, and the avenue de l'Indépendance. I couldn't make out the names of the side streets, so I used my magnifying glass again. Rue Paul-Crampel, where the Studio de Paris was situated in the 1910s, still exists. I didn't simply remember the photograph of my grandfather, I actually saw it come to life. I went deep into the studio, and I thought my grandfather's amused expression was caused by my unexpected intrusion. Who was this Paul Crampel? And who was Barthélemy Boganda? The Dimitris crossroads that Paul-Marie Bourquin had told me about was not on the map.

Studying the map refreshes me after reading the dictionary just as in the past the illustrations in schoolbooks had. I took to illustrating the books that had no pictures in them, drawing in the margins, to the best of my ability, soccer players, cypress trees, and sewing machines. My novels all have wide margins. They seem longer than they really are. Am I incapable of writing a big fat novel like they did so easily in the nineteenth century? According to Georges's theory, which holds that novels are born in railroad stations, this kind of literature must not be highly developed in the Central African Republic. There are absolutely no train tracks.

It's lovely to form sentences in a language that one is just beginning to discover. These sentences are necessarily very simple ones that require no thought and have no literary pretensions. It relaxes the mind to write without trying to express anything, without thinking about oneself, to connect words without any particular reason. It makes the pen lighter and the hand more daring because one is free of the hateful fear of making mistakes. I'm sure the author of the dictionary would easily forgive my clumsiness were I to show him my attempts. Even the French, ordinarily so punctilious about proper usage, forgave me my beginner's mistakes. I misunderstood the word *limitrophe*, "bordering." Because *trophi* means "food" in Greek, I thought that people who lived in *limitrophe* countries lacked food, that there wasn't enough to go around. The allowances that I believe will be made for me, however, don't make me careless. The exercises that I invent—W. J. Reed, alas, doesn't provide any in his book—are rather childish. For example, I make up dialogues between Tarzan and Jane in the tersest style imaginable:

"*Mbi* Tarzan," announces the lord of the jungle.

At the same time, he beats his chest, a habit he inherited from his adoptive parents, which allows Jane to understand the meaning of *mbi*.

"*Mbi* Jane," she answers.

"*Mo* Jane," Tarzan continues, pointing his index finger at the young woman.

"*Mo* Tarzan," she concludes.

I keep coming back to Tarzan, perhaps because without him I would never have become involved in this adventure. It's unlikely that he lived in the Central African Republic. I remember that the tropical forest where he lived was relatively close to the ocean. Still, I think some liberties can be taken with a fictional work. An elephant goes by.

"*Doli*," says Tarzan.

More elephants come running.

"*Adoli*," says Tarzan, who obviously wants to teach Sango to Jane.

The unfortunate beasts are pursued by a band of overzealous hunters in a Jeep.

"*Kutukutu*," says Tarzan.

Professor Archimedes's daughter (how could I have forgotten that Jane's papa had a Greek name?) is no fool. She understands the meaning of *kutukutu* all the more easily because Tarzan pronounces it in a deep voice, as it should be pronounced (*kùtùkùtù*). A procession of Jeeps arrives.

"*Akutukutu*," Jane remarks.

The son of the apes is thrilled. But shortly after the animals and vehicles have disappeared in the depths of the forest, shots ring out.

"*Adoli a kui*," Tarzan states sadly.

One day or another he will explain to Jane that Sango likes

to emphasize the subject when it is a noun by following it with the pronoun *a*. In proper Sango one should say "the elephants they are dead," "my father he is dead," and so on. She takes the initiative to kiss her companion on the cheek to help him forget his sorrow.

"*Angoro*," says Tarzan, his eyes strangely shining.

"That probably means *encore*," Jane thinks immediately, because she speaks perfect French and is aware of its influence on the languages of central Africa. She grants him his wish, and he becomes bolder.

"*Mbi ye mo*," he tells her.

Ye means "to love," "to desire," and also "to want." The expression on his face leaves no doubt as to the meaning of his declaration.

"*Mbi ye mo*," Jane answers.

Despite what this dialogue might suggest, Sango has no real appreciation of short sentences. On the other hand, it can easily do without the verb "to be" in sentences such as "the lion is the king of the jungle" ("the lion king of the jungle"), "my name is Nicolaides" ("my name Nicolaides").

Another exercise that I devised consists in making up book titles. It's relatively easy to do and gives me lots of room to play. A book that deals with life in the past can easily be called *Giriri*, "in the past, once, formerly," or even *Ababa*, "the fathers." Should the teachings of the ancients be perpetuated or resolutely rejected? This subject can be broached in a book entitled *Ababa a kui*, "the fathers have died," or, if one prefers, *Ababa a kui pepe*. I have come up with several titles for love stories: *Awe*, "it's over"; *Mo ye mbi giriri*, "you used to love me long ago"; *Be ti mbi a yeke ti mo*, "my heart is for you"; *Dokotoro a ye apupulenge*, "the doctor loves the girls." I don't think you can give the name of a song to a book. And so I eliminated Enrico Macias's *Apupulenge ti kodoro ti mbi* without much regret really, because I much prefer *Apupulenge ti zua*, "the girls of the island," and, even more, *Apupulenge ti ngu ti Nzapa*, "the girls of the rain." If I were to write a text about my father's death, I would call it *Ngu ti Nzapa*.

Georges likes one-word titles. In January he published a book by Marie-Jo Abdel-Minem called *The Substitute* and another called *Paranoia*, by an elementary school teacher from the Maritime Alps region. I just got off the phone with him a few moments ago; he's off to Trouville. He reminded me about our meeting on August 23. What will I tell him of my work? That I'm making progress? Will I talk to him about my grandfather's letter again? I put it away in a folder where I keep all my identity papers. I often think about that letter. If I had read it, I probably would have forgotten it.

In any case, I will definitely remind Georges of the promise he made me last year to give me the *Grand Robert*. I asked him for it persistently.

"I still have a long way to go in French," I had said to him.

"Those big dictionaries get on my nerves," he'd confided in me. "They make my head spin, like department stores, so that I always wind up forgetting what it is I wanted to find out."

Still, he had committed to sending it to me.

I would be glad to translate the title of one of my books into Sango, but which book? *The Tin Soldier* seems too com-plicated to me. *Letter to Marika* perhaps? I open the dictionary apprehensively, as if I were afraid to face the word "letter." But here it is: *mbeti*. So my book is called *Mbeti na Marika*.

To find myself surrounded by so many Sango words amuses me at times. In the end I'll no longer be able to understand what I'm writing. At other times I'm tormented beneath the weight of my undertaking. Extravagant, enigmatic sentences that I must instantly translate into Sango wake me in the middle of the night: "Having no reason to learn a language is no reason not to learn it."

I'm perplexed by all this mental activity. I remember the wooden blocks I played with as a child. A letter was printed on each of their six sides, but I was completely incapable of forming words. I had to make do with piling them up precariously one on top of the other and watching them fall. My thoughts are as absurd as this game. They make only a slight sound as they tumble down.

Still, I manage to overcome my doubts. I tell myself that my current occupation is really not very far from my work as a novelist. I let myself be carried along by words while I wait for them to consent to reveal the meaning of our journey to me. I hope that Sango will one day have the consideration to explain to me why I learned it.

It was raining cats and dogs when I went to visit Jean at the Cochin Hospital. I was thinking about the big black umbrella that my parents had given me when I left for France. Where had I lost it? I walked along the endless wall outside the Santé prison, and it seemed more sinister than ever. It's so high that you can only see the last floor of the building behind it. I ran until I was out of breath. "They're going to think I escaped. The cops are going to pounce on me." At the entrance to the hospital, a hunchback barred the way.

"And just where is he running to, the gentleman?" he asked me rather sweetly.

I noticed that he had doubled the subject of his question, just like one does in Sango. He was looking hard at me, his head cocked and his eyes wide. "All the hospitals have orders to hire a hunchback."

"I'm going to see my friend Fergusson, a patient of Dr. Préaud's."

"Very well," he sighed, as if relieved.

He held out a photocopy of the layout of the hospital. I didn't want to antagonize him so I took it, but I didn't really need it. At the entrance to the north cemetery in Athens, they also distribute a photocopied layout to the visitors. The burial plots are indicated by boxes with numbers on them. My parents' is number 323.

The Cochin Hospital is a big village made up of prefab buildings and old, run-down extensions of blackened bricks. I was still out of breath as I pushed open the door to Jean's room, on the sixth floor of a recent structure that faces the prison.

"What's the matter?" he said. "Sit down!"

I was having a coughing fit as I sat down in the only chair.

"Should I call the nurse?"

Music wafted softly from a small radio on the night table.

"I had a body scan this morning. All the cancerous cells are dead, totally dead! 'Your skin is like a young girl's, Mr. Fergusson,' the doctor told me. He seemed pleased with himself."

Jean was attached to the IV by two tubes. One was in his right arm beneath a thick layer of gauze held in place by a kind of Band-Aid. The other was attached to his chest where it went through an opening in his pajama top.

"He found some kind of dust in my lungs. He prescribed three chemotherapy sessions for me, I'll do the other two at home. They're going to send me a nurse!"

He removed his blanket with a quick jerk of his feet, revealing his naked legs. He was wearing Y-fronts, like my father's, which surprised me because he takes such good care of his appearance.

"Sandra thinks I'm going to kick the bucket. Sometimes she cries while she's peeling potatoes or washing dishes."

"Is she living with you?"

"She comes over every now and then.... I had my apartment repainted. You wouldn't recognize it. I emptied out the whole thing. I sold all my stuff to a secondhand dealer. I only kept the portrait of my mother and the porcelain candelabra; they were all I had left from the castle in Yorkshire.... I'm even going to sell my bed. I'll put the mattress directly on the floor. Do you think I'm too old to sleep on the floor?"

A nurse's aide came into the room at top speed, covered his legs with the blanket again, and asked him what he wanted for lunch.

"Nothing."

"I'm going to bring you mashed potatoes and some yogurt anyway."

She left us as quickly as she had come.

"Do you remember your father?"

"Barely. He had a limp. My father is a limping shadow. I'm not even sure I can still spell his last name correctly. He was a cabinetmaker who had studied his craft in Lille. He spent his time fixing the parquet floors in the castle. The coroner suspected him of having set the fire to get rid of his wife.... Would anyone set fire to a house whose parquet floors he'd been repairing?"

"Why would he have run away?"

"To forget. One goes away to forget. Do you have any paper on you?"

I only had my checkbook. I gave it to him along with my pen. He made a few signs on the back of the checkbook, with a shaky hand, and showed me the result. He had written his father's name in capital letters: PRZYBYSZEWSKI.

"I don't think I made any mistakes," he said. "For a long time I hoped that my father would show up one way or another, that he would have had the curiosity to see me again. I was intrigued by men who limped in the street."

His bandage had a tendency to come undone. He pushed down hard on both ends of the Band-Aid.

"The first shirts I ever wore were made from strips of gauze," I told him. "At the end of the Occupation, my father had stolen a crate from a German pharmaceutical warehouse, thinking it contained medicine. It was filled with gauze. My mother thought of using it to make shirts. They were very comfortable in summer."

"You must have looked like a burn victim!" he cried.

"Even with my bad memory, I remember how light these shirts were. Are you bored in here?"

"It's the only place I can think in peace. I try to ignore the chatter around me. I often fall asleep amid my thoughts. I let my mind wander. I think of the people I've known. Most of them have aged a lot. More and more my memory is beginning to resemble an old people's home."

He shut off the radio, which was crackling.

"I think about you," he went on. "Sandra is teaching me Italian in exchange for French lessons. I'd really like to be able to speak with her in her own language. But you, with whom are you going to speak Sango?"

"With Tatabou the Sublime! She's the fiancée of one of my childhood heroes, the valiant Gaour, Tarzan's Greek rival."

The nurse's aide returned carrying a tray that she placed on the table.

"It's fresh pineapple!" she insisted.

There was, indeed, between the mashed potatoes and the yogurt, a slice of fresh pineapple. She pushed the table toward Jean.

"Eat!" she ordered him and then cleared out.

Through the window I could see the prison below, a somber, massive shape whose lines were blurred by the rainwater that continued to run down the panes. It looked like the building was wobbling.

"Have you ever heard of Paul Crampel?"

"I think he was an explorer."

"What about Barthélemy Boganda? One of the main avenues in Bangi is named after him."

"He was the head of the national separatist movement. He died young in a bizarre plane crash.... I could tell you a lot more about Bokassa if you wanted, the famous Jean-Bedel Bokassa, who had himself crowned emperor of Central Africa in 1977 with both the consent and the money of the French. He arranged a ceremony modeled on the coronation of Napoleon. Can you imagine the scene David painted taking place in the sports stadium in Bangi? Of course, Bokassa was on excellent terms with Valéry Giscard d'Estaing, who was the French president at the time. Giscard was often invited by him to visit the Central African Republic, and Bokassa offered him amazing gifts. I suppose you remember the diamond affair. It came out right before the 1981 presidential elections when Mitterand beat Giscard. Bokassa's diamonds no doubt had something to do with the Left's victory."

I had the feeling I was reading the back cover of a novel by Alexandre Dumas. "It wasn't Bokassa," I thought, "it was his wife who gave Giscard the diamonds. Then she sent four of her most faithful officers to Paris to get them back. She absolutely had to wear them at the Annual Bangi Ball."

"Bokassa had a wife, didn't he?"

"Her name was Catherine. She was much more reasonable than her husband. France finally dropped him. He had led his country to ruin and drowned the student revolt in blood. He was tried in a local court. Prison unhinged him completely and at the end of his life he thought he was the thirteenth apostle of Christ."

"So there are diamonds in the Central African Republic?" I remarked to conclude.

"They say that Bokassa kept them in jelly jars. That kind of wealth only ever benefits a few people. Ange-Félix Patassé, the current president, is one of Bokassa's ex-prime ministers. The name Jean-Bedel comes from the acronym for John Baptist de La Salle, written on the French calendar as Jean-BdL."

The first thing I saw was the bouquet of flowers that Sandra was carrying in her arms like a baby. I got up to greet her. She must have guessed who I was because she kissed me. Her cheeks were wet. Her arrival was enough to dispel the gloom that pervaded the room, she was a breath of fresh air. She wasn't particularly beautiful, but she had the charm of her youth. You could see it in her gestures, in the way she took off her raincoat and searched for a place to put it down, and of course, in the look in her eyes. She made you feel like seeing everything in a new light. She arranged the flowers in a vase that she had taken from the closet, and then she literally lay down next to Jean.

"You didn't eat anything!" she scolded him. "Aren't you hungry, honey?"

I was embarrassed by her term of affection, which raised a corner of the veil of their intimacy.

"I'm going home."

Despite Sandra's protests, I slipped on my overcoat.

"Do you know how to say "illness" in Sango?" Jean asked me.

In fact I had thought of him when I had read that word in the dictionary.

"*Kobela.*"

"It seems less sinister a word than the French *maladie*."

"In Italian we say *malattia*," Sandra added.

"Well that's exactly why I didn't want to learn Italian," I thought to myself. "It's too close to French. It's like French dressed up in party clothes."

"Current events will force us one day to adopt a bunch of African words, just like we are bringing more and more Arabic words into the language. A short while ago, no one had heard of *intifada* and *jihad*, *ayatollah*, and *mujahidin*. Now we're discovering the Taliban and their schools, the *madrasa*."

"Do French people understand those words?" Sandra asked, surprised.

"Not really. The role of these words is to show us the limits of our knowledge and of our understanding. They are hermetic words that reveal nothing. But they point the way."

Early one morning, a few days after my visit to the hospital, a young delivery boy brought me a very heavy cardboard crate. I signed a receipt for him and then brought the crate into my apartment by pushing it with my feet. I slid it toward my office, as if I had guessed what was in it. Was I in no hurry to open it? I worked slowly and carefully to undo the string wrapped around it. It's probably my father who led me to believe that you never know when you'll need some string. I cut the sticky tape with a craft knife and finally opened the crate.

In front of me was the *Grand Robert*. The first thing I did was to count the number of volumes. I was so excited that I had to start over three times. There were nine of them, all bottle-green. Each spine had two burgundy stickers on it. I immediately called Georges and confessed to him that I was just about to ask him for them at our lunch.

"Well, you needn't bother," he said simply.

"I'm just as excited as when I received the prize from the Académie française."

He didn't remember that one of my novels, *Happy Birthday*, had received one of the many prizes awarded by this institution.

I took the last volume out of the crate with as much care as if it had been made of glass and set it down gently on my desk. The Sango dictionary seemed very thin in comparison. "Here's a language that's still searching for itself next to one that has found itself." I piled the other volumes atop the first one, and then started to wonder where I could put them. Alas, I couldn't see any spot that could possibly hold them. The shelf attached to the wall next to the desk already had several Greek dictionaries on it, the *Petit Robert* dictionary, the old *Larousse* encyclopedia in two volumes, and the new Bescherelle *Art of Conjugating*. And in any case, it wasn't attractive enough. I wasn't about to put the *Grand Robert* on a simple board whose paint was chipping. I thought about emptying out the bookcase with glass doors between the two windows, but the *Grand Robert* deserved more than such an ordinary piece of furniture, with its doors that didn't close properly and its cracked pane of glass. "I should get rid of it."

It didn't take me long to come to a decision. I raced to a furniture store on the boulevard de Grenelle, where I bought a magnificent, white wood bookcase big enough to hold all my books. "The dark green of the dictionary will be perfectly set off by these pale shelves," I thought. The salesman promised to get it to me that very afternoon. It was only 10:10 in the morning.

By 11:30 I had brought the glass-doored bookcase and the other shelving down to the courtyard of my building, and had even plastered the holes I made in the wall when I removed the hardware that had held it in place. I gave myself a little break, sprawling out on the couch whose springs seemed to poke out more than ever. They were piercing through the velour. Several mountains of books surrounded the map of the Central African Republic. The *Robert* had remained on my desk. I was eager to open it, to skim through one or two entries, but I didn't think it was quite time. All the walls, with the exception of a rectangle that had been saved from filth by the glass-doored bookcase, were in an awful state. "I'm going to do what Jean did. I'm going to paint everything over. I couldn't possibly welcome the dictionary into my home any less warmly than he has welcomed a young Italian woman whose French is less than perfect."

It took me about an hour to buy five kilos of white paint, a roller, two liters of white spirit, and a ladder that I carried home on my back. Even though I was exhausted, I immediately set to work, starting with the wall near the desk where I planned to set up the new bookcase. I worked like an automaton, with the kind of astonishing energy you see in actors in silent films. Which is to say that on several occasions I almost fell off my ladder.

Around three o'clock, perhaps because I hadn't eaten anything, perhaps because I had splashed paint all over my curtains, I became completely disheartened. "No matter what I do, my apartment will still be insignificant. The *Grand Robert* deserves a room paneled in dark wood, with upholstered doors and ceilings decorated with chubby cherubs." I was on the verge of tears. Should I move, change neighborhoods? Perhaps settle in Versailles? I lit my pipe, which helped to calm me. I had only one wall left to paint. As I moved the couch, one of its armrests fell off. I called the furniture salesman and managed to convince him to send me, along with the bookcase, the small couch that I had seen in the window.

The deliverymen came at 6:30. There were two of them. I helped them put the furniture together and carry both pieces to their permanent spots. In exchange for a good tip, they were kind enough to take away the old couch, the curtains, and all the boxes. The light from the setting sun colored the walls a lovely ochre.

First I put back the books that were scattered on the rug, leaving an entire shelf free for the *Grand Robert*. When it came time to set it in its place, I wondered if I really had the right to it. I thought back on the little French-Greek dictionary that I had brought in my suitcase when I first came to Paris; it also had a green cover. I used it so often that in just a few months its edges had turned black. It helped me to decipher the newspaper, which I would read scrupulously every night. Had I seen myself as a warrior launching an assault on the French language? The newspaper I used to buy regularly was called *Combat*. "I don't need the French-Greek dictionary any more," I thought. I allowed myself to place the first volume of the *Robert* on the shelf.

I knew I would be in France for a long time. The military junta that had seized power in Greece with the support of the United States was showing no signs of weakening. The books I was dreaming of writing could not be published in my country. I began to dream of them in French. I systematically read other writers who had chosen to express themselves in a foreign language: Beckett, Nabokov, Conrad. I found them to be excellent. I placed the second volume next to the first.

Moving on to the third volume, I recalled the passionate letters I had written to a French woman named Julie a year after having settled in Paris. Every day I would write her a three-page missive. I'm sure these letters were riddled with mistakes, and yet somehow I managed to touch her. I began to write in French before I knew the language.

Julie had a veritable passion for Georges Brassens. She would make me listen to him all day long. The better I grasped the meaning of the words to his songs, the more I appreciated the music. Brassens taught me a host of new words, ones that revealed the great diversity of the fair sex — hussy, shrew, biddy, grisette, wench, vamp, tart. I put the fourth volume on the shelf while humming one of his songs:

> *Elle n'avait pas la tête, elle n'avait pas*
> *L'esprit beaucoup plus grand qu'un dé à coudre,*
> *Mais pour l'amour on ne demande pas*
> *Aux filles d'avoir inventé la poudre*

Which translates roughly as:

> She wasn't bright, her brain was small
> No bigger than a little thimble,
> But in matters of love, really all
> I ask of girls is that they be nimble.

I put my own books in chronological order on the shelf right above the one reserved for the *Grand Robert*. The one whose publication had pleased me the most was the first one, *Monk Gaspard's Three Sisters*, a parody of an adventure novel. It had got three good reviews, the most laudatory in the *Soir de Marseille*, which ended with these words: "Go out and buy *Monk Gaspard's Three Sisters*, it will be money well spent." While I was arranging the fifth volume on the shelf,

I counted my novels: there were six. Without the slightest hesitation, I placed volume six of the *Grand Robert* on the shelf as well.

The seventh, almost entirely devoted to the letter "P," made me think about the portentous premises of the Paris police prefecture where I had to renew my residence permit. Once a year without fail the police would remind me of a truth that I had a tendency to forget: I was still a foreigner. I recalled this painful period when I would constantly reproach myself for having betrayed my culture. Since democracy had been restored in Greece, I no longer had any excuse for neglecting my mother tongue. It wasn't until after I had kept the promise I had made to my mother to translate my first books, and after having written a novel in Greek, that I could again take up the thread of my conversations with the French language without any qualms. I placed the penultimate volume upon the shelf.

I sat at my desk and surveyed the room. The white paint made it appear larger and erased everything, including the memory of the glass-doored bookcase. The new couch, lower and smaller than the old one, barely attracted any attention. It was covered with an ecru comforter that stretched across its back. "I've done my best," I thought as I grasped the ninth volume. I weighed it in my hand. Was it really heavier than the others? Why was I taking so long to put it on the shelf? Was I at a turning point, the meaning of which I hoped to understand by drawing it out? Fatigue on the one hand and the smell of paint on the other were befuddling me. I thought about the Greek words that were contained in the *Grand Robert* and the French ones that could be found in the Sango dictionary. I had the comforting feeling that my affection for Sango was not the sign of a break in my history. Rather, it was simply a continuation of a longstanding curiosity of mine, one that predated even my arrival in France, one that I had felt for the first time in the north cemetery of Athens when I had deciphered the name of Katerina G. Papageorgiou.

I set the final volume upon the shelf. The *Grand Robert* took up over half of it. It was more impressive than ever. I realized that I could finally open it, but what word should I look up? My old fanciful etymology of the word *limitrophe* came to mind, and I pulled down the sixth volume. *Trophe* does indeed come from the Greek *trophein*, "to eat, to nourish oneself," but the Latin root in the word has nothing to do with a lack of any sort. It designates a frontier, a border region. This region is described as "nourishing" because traditionally it was supposed to supply the troops stationed there.

The darkness overtaking the room was making the smell of the paint more and more acrid. I took refuge in the kitchen, carrying the Sango dictionary with me. I set it down only after I had cleaned the table carefully.

"You did a good job," said Alice as she inspected the walls.

I had managed to convince her to come over without too much trouble. She hadn't been over in ages. I told her that I absolutely had to show her what I had done to the place. I am starved for compliments.

"Good job," she says again.

She's standing in the middle of the living room, one step away from the map of Central Africa. I hope she's seen it and that she isn't going to walk on it. She's wearing high-heel sandals, a black mini-skirt, and a khaki-colored shirt. I remain next to the desk. Sango doesn't have a very large vocabulary for describing colors. It uses the same term for brown and for yellow, and the same for dark blue and black. Sometimes it turns to a circumlocution to clarify a difference in hue. So, for example, it likens orangey red to the color of mangoes during rainy season.

"What else is new?" she says.

She seems much better disposed toward me than at our last meeting, in mid-May. I had invited her to the movies to see *The Flame and the Arrow*, a take-off on Robin Hood from the 1950s with Burt Lancaster. She found it childish. I remembered during the movie that Tarzan also had a bow and arrows.

"What's new?" I repeated, like an echo.

I've spent my life sitting on a desk chair. I can't possibly have any news. She moves toward the window, brushing the map. She leans outside, resting her belly on the balustrade. Summer has finally arrived. The sun lights up her hair and places two golden epaulettes on her blouse. I try not to look at her thighs.

"I'm learning Sango."

She bursts out laughing.

"That's not news!"

When had I spoken to her at such length about Sango? Have I started to repeat myself? I have rarely heard her laugh so gaily. Could she have drunk a glass of Burgundy before coming up? She's from Burgundy. She studied midwifery in Dijon. That's about the only thing I know about her past.

"You taught me how to say 'I am only me one': *mbi yeke gi mbi oko*. Isn't that right?"

"Yes, that's right."

"I'll teach her Sango when I've finished learning it. We'll speak to each other only in Sango." How would our relationship evolve if we were to speak to each other in a new language? Would she say more? It seems to me that the innocuous nature of foreign words leads one to chatter more easily, in the same way that money whose real value one doesn't understand leads one to spend more. Alice is not very loquacious. She doesn't like to dwell on her childhood, has rarely spoken to me about her son Gabriel, and has never mentioned her husband. The only subject she willingly discusses is her work in the Port Royal maternity hospital. She hates the fact that the first light newborns see comes from a bank of spotlights, and is fighting for labor rooms to be opened to daylight.

"What else can you say?"

Her skirt is held up by a mere elastic waistband. The large military belt she is wearing over it is purely for decoration. I don't dare approach her though. During the time we were seeing each other on a regular basis, she would only agree to meet me once I had promised I wouldn't touch her. She would pretend to have forgotten that we had already slept together and that I never kept my promises. Sometimes my advances really made her angry, and she'd leave, slamming the door. Did she feel guilty because of her husband? Did she mean to save our relationship from wearing out? She would systematically put up the kind of resistance that other women usually put up only the first time. We were living a timeless adventure, one that perpetually renewed itself. It ended without having aged.

She sat down cross-legged on the couch. My gaze rested on the Sango dictionary, open to page 269. The last word I had underlined was the verb *nzere*, "to please."

"I know how to say 'you please me,' or, more precisely in Sango, 'you are pleasing to my eyes.' Sango makes constant reference to the body and its organs. 'To help' is translated by 'to give the hand,' 'to embrace' is 'to take on one's body,' 'to be impatient' is 'to have a restless heart.' The heart is the seat of both feelings and of intelligence. 'To rummage through one's heart' means 'to think, to reflect.'"

"I didn't ask for a lecture!" she said mockingly.

I ignore her objection:

"The body is omnipresent in speech. When one rests, one says one is resting one's body, when one hides one says one is concealing one's body, when one is covered with sores one specifically says that one's body is covered with sores. A meeting is an assembly of bodies. The question 'How are you?' refers directly to the body, 'How is your body?' I've even gotten to the point where I wonder how Central Africans perceive the pronoun 'I.' Do they first think of their body? What does this word mean to you?"

I sit down next to her. Could my eyes be shining strangely like Tarzan's in the episode I invented? She makes a tiny movement as if she were preparing to get up, but she stays where she is. She doesn't answer my question.

"Say 'you are pleasing to my eyes' in Sango."

I know this sentence perfectly, and yet I hesitate to say it aloud. Am I put off by how long it is? My embarrassment amuses Alice.

"Come on!" she says.

Then her expression changes. She looks at me with compassion.

"*Mo nzere na le ti mbi*," I say in one breath. "*Le* refers to the eyes. Am I pleasing to your eyes? *Mbi nzere na le ti mo*?"

She dodges this question as well.

"Are we going out to eat?" she asks.

"Don't you want to stay here?"

She hesitates now.

"I'm rummaging through my heart," she says. "I suppose you only have spaghetti in the house?"

"I also have tomato sauce and several cans of tuna! And wine!"

73

I feel like it's a holiday. She hangs her belt on the back of her chair and then takes over. I'm enchanted to see her handling my utensils, opening my cupboards, lighting the oven. Things come alive around her. My presence adds no cheer to the places I'm in. I even think it makes them gloomier than when I'm not there.

"I'd like to know more about Africa and Asia, wouldn't you?" she asks.

"Africa seems closer to me, more accessible. The novels I read as a teenager rarely took place in Asia. I never knew what a Chinese puzzle was. I don't even know if you can make up crossword puzzles in Chinese. Africa scares me less."

"What about the lions?"

"Lions are my friends!"

I pour her some wine. She doesn't cover her glass, she doesn't say stop. Will she stay after lunch? She drains the pasta.

"What do they drink in the Central African Republic?"

"My information comes from the dictionary. They drink beer made from millet, and palm wine that they obtain by making an incision at the top of palm trees. It's drunk fresh or fermented with bitter fruit peels. They also drink blood mixed with water to seal a pact."

"And what do they eat?"

She is eating slowly, conscientiously rolling her spaghetti around her fork.

"I haven't seen the word 'pasta' in the dictionary. They don't like chicken eggs. Central Africans refer to white people as 'egg eaters.' There is a fish called 'captain,' *kapitani*, that they catch in the Ubangi, and it's delicious, but some people don't eat it because it might be the incarnation of a dead person. André Gide wrote in his journal that hippopotamus meat is quite popular. Manioc, yams, eggplant, and plantains are among the most common foods. They are fond of caterpillars and grilled termites as hors-d'oeuvres. They make honey and a strange kind of seasoning produced from the ashes of certain plants."

Her attention wanders the more I speak. I notice her coming upon the photograph of my parents that I recently stuck on my refrigerator door. It is from 1947, the year I was born. They are on a ship's bridge, their backs to the sea. They aren't holding hands, yet they are very close to each other. My father's tie, floating in the wind, forms a hyphen between them.

"Shall we rest in the other room?" I ask, trying to conceal my excitement.

"If you promise me. . . ," she says without looking at me.

Of course I promise her. The daylight filtering through the bedroom's closed shutters marks the ceiling with luminous streaks. We remain motionless on the bed, eyes staring at the ceiling. Alice didn't get undressed, didn't even take off her sandals. Then we remember. Each of our gestures takes us further back in time. They are gestures we have known forever. Our past shrinks at incredible speed. Soon all that is left is the present moment.

Alice is asleep. Her cheeks are the color of mangoes during rainy season. Is she still living with her husband? She rarely speaks about her life because her life is nothing like her.

She wears no rings, not even a wedding ring. She has large hands with slender fingers. What made her decide to become a midwife? She frequently spends sleepless nights at the hospital. My father was convinced that he would die in his sleep. He would wake up several times a night to reassure himself that he was still alive. He thought that the night would betray him. But it was finally day that played the trick on him. He died at ten in the morning.

I'm starting to get restless. I steal out of bed, go smoke my pipe in the living room, and then fetch the Sango dictionary. I get back in bed with it. Alice hasn't budged. I invent new sentences: *Ngu ti Nzapa a nzere na mbi pepe*, "the rain doesn't please me," *Sandra a nzere na le ti Jean*, "Sandra is pleasing to Jean's eyes," *Alice nzere na le ti baba ti mbi giriri*, "Alice used to be pleasing to my father's eyes," *Mbi nzere na mbi pepe*, "I don't please myself." I skip over *nzia*, a tropical plant whose Latin name (*phyllanthus reticulates*) makes it even more inaccessible. The fact that it is used in traditional pharmacopoeia to heal purulent wounds doesn't seem to me to be a sufficient reason to memorize it. I do, however, take note of the adverb *nzoni*, "well, " "fine." The fact that it resembles *nzere* will allow me to memorize it quite easily, I'm sure. It makes me want to take up my exercises once again: *Mbi yeke nzoni*, "I am well," *Mbi yeke nzoni na zua ti mbi*, "I am doing well on my island," *Adoli a yeke nzoni na Beafrika*, "Elephants are fine in the Central African Republic."

"Are you talking to yourself?"

Her voice startles me. I quickly place the book on the floor.

"Do you want to know how to say 'I'm fine with you' in Sango?'"

I lean over toward her shoulder to kiss her, but she pulls away. She draws the sheet up, covering herself to the neck.

"You took my clothes off again," she says very quietly. "You really can't be trusted."

I stroke her hair. I realize that this gesture bothers her. I know it perfectly, as if I were in her place. I feel the same irritation even though I don't understand it.

"You aren't fine? Do you want to know how to say 'I'm not fine' in Sango?"

"No."

I'm disappointed. I really would like to say *Mbi yeke nzoni pepe* to her, to talk to her as well about the negating adverb that comes at the end of sentences.

"I don't want to be burdened with new words. The words I know give me enough nightmares."

To what sort of nightmares is she referring? What are the words that trigger them? It's useless to question her. She sits up in bed, holding the sheet securely in front of her breasts.

"The only thing you've talked to me about since I got here is Sango," she says bitterly.

"I'm sure I have a tendency to dwell on this subject more than necessary, probably because I don't know it well. It seems to me that one is more inclined to speak about things one knows nothing about. One needs to surprise one's own self."

She gets up, taking the sheet with her, and modestly wraps it around her.

"I'm leaving. I'll let you get back to work."

"But I'm in no hurry, Alice. You can stay. We'll go to a restaurant for dinner."

The truth is I don't want her to stay. Her hypersensitiveness forces me to weigh each of my words, to calculate my gestures, which would wear me out completely if our tête-à-tête were to go on. And it would be very disagreeable to me to have to spend an entire evening without saying a single word about the language that constantly occupies my thoughts. I would feel like I was cheating on it.

Alice leaves the bedroom, taking her clothes with her. The water in the bathroom begins to run. My naked body on the bed is a sorry sight. I observe the folds forming under my arms. My father had the same ones. The color of my skin, a very pale yellow that turns to gray in spots, also makes me think of him.

Edgar Rice Burroughs stated that the best way to defend oneself in the presence of a lion was to play dead. Is this true? I have only seen lions in the movies, on television, or on bas-reliefs from antiquity. Above the main door to the palace in Mycenae two lionesses are portrayed. According to mythology, Hercules killed a lion in Nemea. Am I to believe that there really were lions in Greece in those faraway times when statues had not yet become stiff, and when nymphs and ephebes roamed the streets? The memories that I still have of Greek statuary make the image in front of my eyes more pitiable still. I try to console myself by thinking that the majority of ancient works have come down to us missing an arm, a leg, and — always — the sex organs. In the early Christian era, they fell victim to the same kind of religious fervor that rages today in Afghanistan to the detriment of Buddhist relics. Thank God the first Christians didn't have dynamite. Alice is standing entirely dressed in the doorway.

"Still in bed?"

She tosses me the sheet.

"Can I open the shutters?"

The traces of light have vanished from the ceiling. I don't see them anywhere. And yet the sun is still in the sky. It's as if it hasn't moved since late morning. Alice goes back to the window, exactly as she had done in the living room. I have the impression that her profile has simply become slightly darker.

"Your father would consult the English dictionary before calling me. He would draw up a list of the words he intended to use. One day he said to me that our trades were the exact opposites of each other, that we were posted at either end of life, I at its beginning and he at its end."

I had no idea that my father could express such a complex thought in English. The letters I used to send to Julie came to mind. They had forced me to make enormous progress in French. My father had probably been more attached to Alice than I realized.

"He didn't only call you on your birthdays?"

"He must have called me about once a month. On my birthday, he would call very early in the morning so he could be the first to wish me happy birthday. You don't remember the date of my birthday, do you?"

"You know I forget everything, Alice."

"That's okay. See you later."

"She's in a hurry to get outside. . . . She'll feel better once she leaves the building. She'll be able to breathe better."

"Stay where you are," she adds with authority. "You don't need to walk me out."

"Can I just tell you one last thing in Sango?"

"Go ahead," she says softly.

"When one asks a woman who is leaving when she'll be back, one asks, 'How many times will you sleep before you return?'"

Her face is devoid of all expression. She quickly crosses the room. I hear the muffled sound of her footsteps on the carpet, then the noise of the closing door. I realize that my father was almost as silent as Alice. I immediately reproach him for it:

"You left me only one letter, it isn't even from you, and I may not even read it," I murmur.

He has trouble opening his eyes. Finally he looks at me. I don't want to hurt him.

"Rest now. We'll talk about it another time."

He lowers his eyelids halfway as a sign of agreement. Suddenly a dark foreboding makes me get out of bed. I race into the living room and look at the map of Central Africa. What I feared has indeed happened: Alice's heel has made a hole that resembles a volcano crater in the paper. Luckily, it's beyond the country's borders, on the top of the map, in Chad.

I found three words that Sango and Greek have in common. Two are from the Arabic: *dunya*, "the world" (another of Vamvakaris's songs, in which he uses this word, came to mind: "All the hooligans in the world/Show me their affection"), and *sandugu* (*sendouki* in Greek), "crate" or "trunk." The third, *politiki*, "politics," is of course authentically Greek. Alas in Sango it has taken on the sense of "demagogy," "lies." That just goes to show you that the language is not lacking in critical intelligence. This is confirmed by the fact that, in the early 1950s when France was governed by the RPF (Rally for the French People), General de Gaulle's party, concessionary companies continued to act as ruthlessly in the colonies as they had in André Gide's time, and the initials RPF gave birth to the word *erepefu*, "forced labor."

The dictionary teaches me as much about the country as it does about the language. I have the impression of browsing through a tourist guidebook. I'm beginning to have a pretty clear idea of the Central African house. It's neither very solid nor very watertight. Usually it is built of clay bricks and has only a thatched roof. The inhabitants sleep more often on matting than in beds. Marcel Alingbindo describes the family at length. In general, there are about twenty children, who do not all have the same mother. The men can marry several women, one after the other. Sometimes the children of one woman have different fathers as well. Sango distinguishes among children who are full siblings, half-siblings on the father's side, and half-siblings on the mother's side. It has specific words for a paternal aunt, a maternal uncle, and even for the husband whose wife has a twin sister. The preciseness of the language in matters of the family, however, is far from perfect. The terms *baba* and *mama* are not limited to parents. They are also applied to the father's brothers and the mother's sisters.

What are the lives of all these children like? One of their favorite games is to go in the river and beat the water's surface with their open palms. This apparently produces a drum-like sound. Do they still undergo the rites of excision or circumcision? The author of the dictionary states that their preparation for this operation includes learning a secret language. Their parents apparently have trouble raising them, for many of them live on the street, in gangs, searching for odd jobs and becoming petty thieves. They sleep under the stars.

The Catholic and Protestant churches have a large presence, yet people still believe that sorcerers are inhabited by the spirit of evil, the *likundu*. The battle against sorcerers is waged by medicine men, the *nganga*, who also serve as doctors. They have a strange custom known as the "trial by poison," in which poison is administered to individuals suspected of witchcraft. Only the guilty die. Divination is practiced using cowries. They are tossed on a table and their position is examined. Old women from the region of Delphi do the same thing, using fava beans instead of shells.

The sentences cited in the dictionary and in the textbook to clarify the meaning of a word or a grammatical rule provide a very somber picture of the country. At first I didn't really pay attention to what they were saying. I was happy just to learn the word or the rule. In the end, though, I noticed their content.

They conjure up a population that is suffering and sickly ("A certain serious illness is afflicting a small number of people," "His entire face is swollen," "All of them have bilharziasis"), penniless ("I don't even have enough money to buy salt," "He is dressed in rags"), on the verge of despair ("I shall die from misery"). They report all kinds of catastrophes ("While they were putting out a fire in one house, another hut collapsed and caught fire next door"). W. J. Reed cites the following dialogue: "Did you earn much from your cotton this year?" "Not a cent, the insects ate everything!"

It's hard not to believe in the *likundu* when one is struck by so much adversity. The poison concocted by the medicine men is extremely violent ("The poison made them tremble violently"). In truth the innocent have absolutely no hope ("He drank the poison so he will die").

Some Central Africans feel sorry for their own people ("Grandmother, why are you crying like that?" "I will cry all the way to the village"). Others recall the wrongdoings of the whites ("They tore Africa to shreds, like hyenas"). Most have a tendency to get all worked up ("He tore the loincloth in anger," "He went to get a club"). Even spiders lose their tempers ("The spider got angry").

The stories these short sentences recount can only end badly: "And the people who were there at the time began to strike each other with knives in a free-for-all." "Once I've killed him, I can throw him in the brush, can't I?" someone asks.

The quotations that show wisdom ("The world has no owner"), that teach patience ("We shall construct our country little by little"), that demonstrate a deep respect for life ("Every person is a person") are few and far between.

The words make me think of immigrants who constantly rehash their memories: they speak to me about their country without managing to communicate their nostalgia or their distress. Jean is right to say that they all point in a certain direction. Rather than satisfying my curiosity, they whet it. They provide information, but they don't deliver up their secrets. Each new word I discover offers me a tiny enigma.

So what do I need to do to learn Sango properly? Do I go there, to the heart of Africa? I feel completely incapable of making such a decision. "I'd like a ticket to Bangi" seems an impossible sentence for me to say.

Still, I dreamed of Africa a short while ago. I was on the bank of a river in which a crocodile was swimming. A man was seated astride its back—a fat, aging but still vigorous soldier with a crew cut. I thought he would quickly fall into the water and be devoured. I felt sorry for him. He was armed with a knife, yet he couldn't manage to drive it into the hard carapace. So he started attacking the eyes, twenty times he plunged his knife into the animal's eyes. He succeeded in tearing out the eyeballs. I saw them dangling miserably from their sockets. I felt sorry for the crocodile.

4

One night, when I was tired from working so diligently for so long and felt not only like closing my books but like tossing them out the window—I imagined they would open as they fell, like birds spreading their wings—the telephone rang.

It was the evening of July 13. More than two months had gone by since I had begun learning Sango. I was fed up with this language, its syntax, its quirks. Its exoticism had quenched my thirst for novelty; my beginner's vanity was satisfied. The bet I had made seemed so senseless that I avoided asking myself if I had won. I was more than tired, I was exhausted, demoralized.

I had finished reading the dictionary and the textbook and had taken hundreds of notes. I was sitting at my desk but no longer working. I was thinking about the sketches I used to draw after each game of my favorite soccer team, the Athens AEK, so I could remember the goals that had been made. I would draw the players and indicate by a broken line the passes that had been exchanged before one of them sent the ball deep into the net. Sometimes the opposing team's goalie would be fooled by a topspin and make a dive on the wrong side. I always need a piece of paper and a pencil to understand things.

I put aside my notes and the two books, freeing up the space in front of me, as if I were about to move on to something else. In truth, I was content simply to contemplate this empty space for a few moments. Then I raised my eyes to the windows, which offered a more interesting scene. The wind that had risen at nightfall was making my new curtains ripple, filling them with air and then suddenly drawing them outside. I saw them fluttering about like handkerchiefs. It was as if my apartment were leaving the neighborhood, waving goodbye to the buildings across the way.

It was ten o'clock. I remained motionless, my hands crossed on the desk. Sometimes near large museums one sees people disguised as statues, dressed in white sheets, hair and face white as well, waiting for handouts from tourists. I also thought of the stiff Evzone guards at the Tomb of the Unknown Soldier in front of the Greek Parliament building. "I'm looking for a family," I thought. My solitude weighed on me, without arousing in me the slightest desire. I could hear the distant sounds of the outdoor balls organized for the July 14 celebrations. The music didn't cheer me up at all. It merely drew my attention to the heaviness in my legs and whispered insulting comments about my age. Already the media were describing in detail the grandiose celebrations lined up for the eve of the year 2000.

I got it into my head that I was like a sentence without a verb, incapable of taking action, amorphous. Verbs are worked-up little military leaders. They are the ones that call words to arms, that lead sentences to battle. They see danger everywhere. The verb "to have" doesn't exist in Sango. It is replaced by the verb "to be" followed by the preposition *na*, "with." "To have quinine" becomes "to be with quinine"; whereas in French one says *avoir faim*, "to have hunger," in Sango one says "to be with hunger"; the French *avoir froid*, literally "to have cold," is said in Sango "to be with the cold," *a yeke na de*. Was I really ready to give up Sango? I looked at the dictionary as if I were waiting for it to respond. And, in a certain sense, I can say that it did, for it was exactly then that Marcel Alingbindo called me.

My first reaction was to stand, the way you do in the presence of a distinguished person. But I was too stunned to move.

"Paul-Marie Bourquin told me that you're working on Sango and that you'd like to meet with me."

His voice was strong and rough. It threw the words into relief. It was the voice of the dictionary.... It had broken its silence to reward me for my efforts.

"Unfortunately, I live in Poitiers and I'm leaving the day after tomorrow for Spain. I'm teaching a class in general linguistics at the University of Barcelona's summer school. I'll be gone until the fifteenth of September."

My sad mood and my weariness had disappeared as if by magic. I felt myself filled with the same intrepid ardor that dangerous situations inspire in the heroes of novels.

"Would you agree to see me tomorrow?" I ventured. "I think I could be in Poitiers around noon. I just have a few questions for you."

It didn't take him long to make up his mind.

"Come for lunch," he said. "Do you mind eating with my family? Do you like fish?"

I was tempted to tell him I like everything, fish of course, but also hippopotamus meat, plantains, manioc paste, and even grilled termites. He suggested that I take the 9:50 from

86

the Montparnasse station for La Rochelle, and he gave me his address.

"My house isn't far from the station," he said.

For a moment I thought about running to join the people dancing for the fourteenth of July, but it seemed wiser to reread my notes, which took me until 2:30 in the morning. At eight o'clock, when the alarm clock rang, I had already been up for a long time. I was the first passenger to board the 9:50 for La Rochelle.

We are sitting in front of his computer on the second floor. He intends to create a website for teaching Sango. He shows me the course he is developing, which will be spread over thirty lessons. He's only up to lesson number three. It begins with the rule for forming the plural: "The plural of nouns is formed by adding the prefix *a-*." There follow numerous examples, a few of which I already know: *ababa, adoli, akutukutu*. The doubts I had about the existence of this language are now gone forever. The words that scroll across the screen seem much more alive than the ones I read in the dictionary. I have the feeling of reaching the depths of the language.

Marcel Alingbindo is proofing his copy very attentively, through gold-framed glasses. From time to time he taps away at his keyboard to correct an accent, add a hyphen, shift a term. Every time he forgets my presence, I allow myself to glance around the bedroom. I've noticed a pair of yellow leather slippers beneath the sofa bed. They are embroidered with what looks like a lizard. A blackboard is resting against a wall. On it are traces of chalk, some better erased than others. "He's teaching Sango to his children," I think. A child of about eight had opened the door for me. He studied me solemnly before mov-

87

ing aside to let me in. A good portion of the wall to the right of the window is taken up by fabric with a print that represents a couple aboard a pirogue. The man is pushing the small craft forward with a long stick that he thrusts into the reddish waters. He is standing in the rear while the woman is sitting in front. She is equipped with an open parasol. The sky is also red. A crucifix made of black wood is suspended above this image.

The third lesson is drawing to a close. It ends with the saying with which I am familiar, "Every person is a person," *zo kue zo*. Marcel Alingbindo turns to me with a broad smile. On his thin face, with its deep wrinkles and the dark shadows on his cheekbones and temples, this smile attains a surprising brightness.

"Can you say something to me in Sango?" he asks.

His invitation doesn't embarrass me inordinately. I have visited his dictionary so frequently that I feel somewhat like one of his students. Still, the sentences that come to mind—"You are pleasing to my eyes," "I am only me one," "The doctor likes girls"—seem out of place to me. I finally choose the one that I learned first:

"*Baba ti mbi a kui.*"

I immediately see that he has understood me. He is wearing the same dejected expression that my father had when he would greet a widow or an orphan.

"Is that true? You've lost your papa?"

"Yes, on March seventh. I also know the adjective *mbasambara.*"

I think of Snow White. Can her name be translated into Sango? The word "snow" is not in the dictionary.

"Get used to paying attention to the tones," he advises me. "They are just as much a part of the language as the vowels are. If you have doubts, remember most syllables are low. You don't have to strain your voice: you put the low tone at the level that works for you. The interval between two levels is not fixed the way it is in music. It can be greater than the one that separates two notes. The tones produce a certain melody."

He takes up his pad and a pen. While he is writing, I see the child who opened the door for me reflected in a corner of the screen. He's walking on tiptoe. I don't turn around so as not to betray his presence. He comes up to the couch, grabs the slippers, and disappears just as discreetly.

Marcel Alingbindo shows me the sentence "*Bàbá tí mbi à kúi*" accented correctly.

"Here you have a low syllable, two high ones, and a middle one," he says, pointing them out with his pen. "Then another low one, a high one, and a low one."

He mumbles the sentence without articulating the words, like you would mumble the lyrics to a song that you have forgotten.

"Can you hear the little melody? We could easily exchange commonplaces simply by whistling. But that would require a good knowledge of the tones. Alas, these days no one pays them any mind. The language is becoming impoverished; it is growing flat, boring. The tones express a kind of joyfulness."

The tune he hummed nonetheless seemed rather sad to me, but I refrain from telling him so.

Bursts of laughter can be heard downstairs. I imagine that the mischievous child put on his father's slippers to amuse his brothers and sisters. At the same time a military march fills the air. They're probably watching the July 14 parade on television.

"The course I'm working on is both for foreigners who are attracted to our language and for those Central Africans who don't know it well. Mathilde Bourquin must have told you that

Sango has never been taught in the schools. Young people have always been educated exclusively in French. During the colonial era, students who were foolish enough to express themselves in Sango were punished, forced to wear a bone around their neck. This tradition went on until recently. The political class is convinced that Central Africa needs the French language in order to become a modern country. Students are taught that their mother tongue belongs to the past."

"It took Greek intellectuals a long time to win acceptance for the spoken language."

"But our writers express themselves only in French! They dream of being published in Paris, and they read the literary supplements in French newspapers. Very few texts exist in Sango, with the exception of the Bible. I just finished translating the *Declaration of Human Rights*. I'm constantly forced to invent new words. Because it has not been taught in the schools, Sango is behind the times, though not as much as the regional languages in France. In the 1981 elections, candidates who held their meetings in French were booed. Both languages are used on the radio and on television."

Both Greek and French make the writer's job easier. They have witnessed the birth of enough texts to understand the writer's hesitations and torments. They offer writers solutions, point out paths, and help them to get oriented in the darkness. They are good company and give good advice. How can one express oneself in a language that asks itself more questions than it can provide answers for, a language that is still searching for words? More talent is probably needed to write in Sango than in French or in Greek.

"How do you go about making up words?"

"I let myself be guided by the evolution of the language. I only speed it up a little. *Senda*, 'science,' is used to form several compound nouns. I allowed myself to add *senda-be*, 'cardiology,' *senda-ngu*, 'hydrology,' *senda-ngu-Nzapa*, 'pluviometry,' *senda-Nzapa*, 'theology.' I work in conjunction with journalists and academics in Bangi. We test our neologisms on their respective publics. For example, the noun *bakari* that I invented when I was writing the dictionary with Mathilde is already part of everyday language."

What's happening downstairs? I hear bickering, galloping, doors slamming, objects being knocked over. Marcel Alingbindo hears none of it, or perhaps he's just used to all the commotion. I'd like to start a family just to get used to the sound of children's laughter.

"When we had finished we realized that we didn't have a term for 'dictionary.' And we absolutely needed one because the title of the work had to be in both French and Sango. Then I remembered the stories recounted in my village about a genie in the forest with a big head who was supposed to know everything. His name was Bakari. So we translated 'dictionary' as *bakari*. Obviously we were risking being disowned by speakers of Sango, but as I already told you, they didn't disown us."

He reminds me of a child who has pulled off a good trick. I imagine him on a bank of the Ubangi trying out boats he has made on the water. What happens to the rejected words that no one wanted? There is probably a layer of silt at the bottom of languages.

"We tried to get rid of some of the foreign words that we use, but it's not always easy. The terms *buku*, 'book,' and *kombuta*, 'computer,' which are English, seem to have taken root in the language."

I realize that I am capable of saying "my book is finished," *Buku ti mbi awe*. My writings are merely efforts to define a word that escapes me.... I need to write pages and pages precisely because I don't know that word.

"Marcel!"

Is it his wife who's calling him? It's 1:30. I planned to take the 2:50 back to Paris. Has he forgotten that we were supposed to eat together? He gets up reluctantly, checks that his printer has paper in it.

"I'll make you a copy of my course."

He writes various telephone numbers on his pad: that of his home, his office at the CNRS in Paris, the place where he'll be staying in Barcelona, and finally, his cell phone number.

"Starting in October, I'll be spending two days a week in Paris."

Where will I be in October?

"Don't hesitate to call me whenever you need me. I'll gladly read your manuscript. I'm not asking what sort of text you're going to write, maybe you yourself don't even know yet. I trust you. Paul-Marie sent me *The Tin Soldier*. Yvonne is reading it. Are you familiar with Etienne Goyémidé's *The Silence of the Forest*? It's one of the best Central African novels. The story takes place in the rain forest, in the land of the Pygmies. I'd like to translate it into Sango."

"Marcel!"

The voice has become urgent.

"Coming, coming," he says very softly.

He's only happy in his office. He seems bored in the other rooms. There's nothing to do in them. Professor Archimedes, Jane's father, was so absorbed in observing nature that he never noticed what was going on around him. What was Tarzan's relation to the Pygmies? Did he get along with them?

The wooden staircase that leads down to the first floor is as narrow as the one in my parents' house. I recall that the second stair from the top creaked loudly. I would step over it when I came home late at night, but my mother always heard me. When will I go to Athens to empty out their house and put it up for sale? I'll give the furniture and the clothing to people from the neighborhood. I won't keep much besides papers and photographs. The whole thing won't take long.

No one is in the living room. The television is off. The only disorderly element I see is a metallic curtain rod that's missing one of its supports and is gently dangling in the void. A muslin curtain is hanging from it. The furniture is modest. Everything here leads me to believe that CNRS researchers are paid a minimum.

"All we have is this language," Marcel tells me earnestly. "If it dies, we're lost. It alone knows who we are, and it reminds us of it each morning. Without it we are doomed to be woken by foreign voices."

Yvonne serves the children, who are sitting quietly around the kitchen table. She's dressed in an unflattering orange bou-bou. She is much stronger than her husband, much smaller, much younger too, but she has the same smile.

"Did Marcel overwhelm you?" she asks. "When he gets started speaking about Sango, there's no stopping him."

She rolls her r's much more distinctly than her husband does. "They're not the same ethnicity.... They met on a stormy day, they were seeking shelter beneath the same mango tree. The rain brought them together."

"Let me introduce you to Mr. Nicolaides, a great writer," Marcel announced solemnly.

The children respectfully shake my hand. The two elder daughters, who are sixteen and seventeen, are Marie-Christine and Cécile, the two boys, who are just a bit younger, Gilbert and Thierry, and their little brother, Louis. On the whole, I find that these typically French names don't suit them at all, no more than Marcel and Yvonne are suitable names for their parents. And yet the name Louis seems perfect for a little slipper thief. I take advantage of this ceremony to examine the dishes on the table discreetly: I recognize the plantains and the gelatinous heap of manioc. The main dish is composed of a mixture of cooked spinach and fried fish. Was it for me that Yvonne prepared a bowl of rice? Marcel places me at one end of the table, between Yvonne and Marie-Christine, and sits down at the other.

"You must get good fish in Greece," Yvonne comments.

"Shush, Mama," says Louis authoritatively. "Papa is saying the blessing."

With his eyes closed, Marcel is praying aloud. He is expressing his gratitude to the Lord and asking for His protection. He asks Him to come to the aid of all the wretched of the earth, and in particular to help the thousands of sick people dying every day in Africa for lack of medical attention. His wife and children repeat each sentence he pronounces in unison. Louis is watching me out of the corner of his eye to see if I am following along. My father also used to recite a short prayer before tucking into his meal, but it was silent. He would stare at something for a few seconds—generally he would choose the knob of the kitchen door—and then he would make the sign of the cross. Marcel's last words leave me totally stunned:

"And we pray, oh Lord, that you will give our friend Mr. Nicolaides here the inspiration necessary to carry out his work on our language."

I lowered my head, not knowing what else to do. I'd like to confess to him that I have no work in progress. And yet he seems to have such faith in my project that he makes me wonder what my real intentions are. Surely I'll want to recount this scene one day.

"And we pray, oh Lord…," his family repeats.

Everything seems worthy of being told, including the "pop" that Marcel causes when he uncorks the bottle of wine. The children are drinking Coke. "I'm involved in a story over which I have no control. It's moving forward on its own…. All I need to do is keep my eyes open."

"Are you familiar with African cuisine?" Yvonne asks me.

"Not at all."

She shows me how to make little balls of manioc. The paste sticks to my fingers. It is much more compact than I thought. The spinach is not spinach. The fish is delicious. Could it be the famous "captain fish"? In any event, it comes from Bangi, shipped by air by one of Marcel's other sons. I learn that he has three more children in Bangi, no doubt from another wife — the son who sent the fish, who is a lawyer, and two daughters who are already mothers themselves.

"I have twelve grandchildren!" he tells me.

How old can he be? The boys eat quickly. They have a soccer match at 3:30, and Louis wants to go with them. The girls are in a hurry, too. The children are involved in other stories, stories that barely intersect with mine.

"I'm really enjoying *The Tin Soldier*," Yvonne says. "Do you know who Martine reminds me of? Of Cécile! When she was little, she would spend hours at The Rainbow, the big toy store in Poitiers!"

Cécile looks down. Why do they live in Poitiers? I avoid asking superfluous questions so as not to waste the little bit of time I still have at their house. I hope that Marcel will get just as much pleasure from reading my novel and will translate it into Sango. I will become so popular in Bangi that they'll name an intersection after me. The remotest villages will clamor for me to visit. During a book signing in the middle of the forest, I'll see appear before me a white man with splendid muscles, wearing an animal-skin loincloth. He will have a few wrinkles, and his jet-black hair will have grayed slightly, but he will be easily recognizable nonetheless.

"*Mo* Tarzan!" I will say, my heart in my throat.

"*Mo* Nicolaides!" he'll shout, thrilled to meet me at last.

I dip my little ball of manioc into a blackish sauce. Yvonne warned me that it was strong. It's not strong, it's fearsome.

"How do you say Snow White in Sango?" I ask Marcel, trying to breathe in as much air as possible.

"Excellent question," he says. "We don't have a word for 'snow.' With what could we replace it? Think, children! How would you explain what snow is to someone who has never seen it? I'm speaking to you, Marie-Christine!"

His eldest daughter is obviously somewhere else.

"Are you sleeping, big sister?" Thierry teases her.

"I know who she's dreaming about!" says Louis.

"I have no idea!" she says, exasperated.

"You'd invite him to take a look in the fridge, by Jove!"

"By Jove" reminds me of Georges Brassens. Could it be that Marcel came to France at the same time I did? He never betrayed his mother tongue. But the switch to another culture may also be seen as an homage paid to the open spirit of one's original culture. I could never have adapted so well to French if my mother tongue hadn't at least been open to dialogue. Louis lets out a shout. I suppose someone just kicked him under the table. His father continues, unperturbed:

"The snow-like powder that forms on the walls of the freezer has a name in Sango: it's called "dust from the cold." I think the easiest thing would be to translate Snow White as Dust from the Cold. The story would be titled *Dust from the Cold and the Seven Dwarves*."

"Wouldn't it be better to say *Dust from the Cold and the Dwarves Seven?*" I asked.

"Indeed it would, for if as a rule adjectives are placed before nouns, numeric adjectives come after the nouns to which they refer."

I'm the only one listening to him. I eat a plantain, but my mouth is in such a state of shock that the plantain has no taste. Louis slides down to the edge of the seat to try and return the kick that he got. All I can see of him is his round head above his empty plate.

"That kid is a real bag of vices," Marie-Christine cries with indignation.

I wasn't familiar with that expression. Was it taken directly from Sango?

"You don't speak Sango with the children?"

The little boy finally gets permission to follow his brothers to the soccer field. The girls also get up from the table. They all shake my hand again, except Louis, who comes toward me with his head bent forward. I kiss him on his frizzy hair.

"You didn't say the prayer," he mutters.

I ask him, just as discreetly, the following question:

"Can you tell me what you did with the slippers?"

He runs off. I was not nearly as impudent when I was his age. I behaved in school. My mother had convinced me that my future depended on my grades. I would hide my uneasiness. I never openly made fun of the professors, the way the students who were better off than I did. In France I rarely did anything foolish either. I understood almost immediately that immigrants' misdemeanors cause disproportionate reactions, alarm the neighbors, arouse the indignation of the police, and inspire long disquisitions in the press.

"Marcel gives them a Sango lesson every evening. But they know French so much better. The three boys were born in France. They have no need of Sango here. They're learning it to please us because they care about us. French assails us from all directions. When Marcel and I are alone, we speak half in Sango and half in French. Isn't that so, Marcel?"

He comes and sits near us, in the chair where Marie-Christine had been.

"It's difficult to resist the language of the place one lives," he says. "Didn't you write some of your books in French?"

"I write the first version in the language of my characters. I need to stay as close to them as possible in order to imagine their story. I'm naïve enough to think that they really exist. Nonetheless, I didn't learn French passively. I had to force myself to learn it as quickly as possible."

"I assume that you didn't know it very well when you first came to France. Yvonne and I had studied it in school, in Bangi. We also had to force ourselves to learn it since it wasn't our parents' language. In truth, we didn't have a mother tongue. Sango was denigrated by a school system that, at the same time, constantly reminded us that French would never be anything but a foreign language to us. Children should not be lied to."

One of Manolis Anagnostakis's poems came to my mind. The poet advises parents to stop telling their children stories about monsters and other such nonsense, and to tell them the truth instead. Anagnostakis stopped writing when he was very young. He says that poets, like soccer players, should retire young. He belongs to a generation of people who agreed to many sacrifices in order to free Greece, before and after World

War II, and he suffered many disillusions. He gave up writing because he was no longer sure of anything.

"The French, however, were quite good at resisting the languages of their colonies," he remarked bitterly. "Do you know how many African words are recorded in the *Robert*? Only twenty-seven, the best known being 'chimpanzee' and 'cola,' the seed used to make Coca-Cola. Sometimes I tell myself that France sent only the deaf and the blind overseas because no one ever realized that the indigenous peoples misinterpreted the meaning of the death's head found on poisonous products. To an African, this drawing represents a happy man, showing all his teeth as he laughs. The French never noticed that this is how black people laugh."

And as if to persuade me of the validity of his point of view, he once again graced me with his splendid smile. Then he turned to Yvonne:

"I wouldn't go through all this trouble to teach the children Sango if I thought they would have no use for it. On the contrary, I think it will be very useful to them when they decide to decipher their history. One day they will stop, surprised, before a large mirror like the ones you see in hotel lobbies. Only Sango will be able to speak to them in the words they need to hear."

Yvonne says goodbye to me in a strange way: twice she touches my right temple with her forehead, and the left temple only once.

"We'd really love to visit your country!" she confides in me. "But for now we don't foresee going anywhere because of my asthma."

I regret having lit my pipe more than once during lunch. Did they choose to live in Poitiers because the air is better there than in Paris? I recall that Mathilde Bourqin had respiratory problems as well.

Yvonne adds, "You didn't eat a thing!"

Marcel's car, an old gray Pontiac, is parked right in front of the living room window where the curtain rod was falling down. One of the slippers is lying next to the rear wheel of the vehicle. This one is not decorated with a lizard, but with a donkey. I didn't know that this animal, so popular in Greece, could also be found in Africa. I'll feel less disoriented than I thought in Central Africa, should I decide to go there. Marcel gets into the car without noticing the slipper and takes off at top speed because my train is leaving in ten minutes. I begin to imagine that while I was gone my notes on Sango gave birth to a short, original, and profound text that I'll be able to show to my publisher.

In three minutes we're in front of the station. I dissuade Marcel from getting out of the car.

"Are there any Sango words among those twenty-seven terms that can be found in the *Robert*?

"Not a one.... Keep me informed about your work. Our language needs people to speak about it."

I allow myself to take leave of him in the same way Yvonne had said goodbye to me, gently brushing his face twice on one side, once on the other. I stay on the sidewalk until the Pontiac pulls away. Only then do I see the second slipper: it's sitting on top of the trunk. If the jolts and bumps had been going to make it fall, it wouldn't still be there.

The bar car is as empty as it was when I came. France doesn't travel in space on July 14, only in time. As we leave the city, on a street corner I spy a man in a dark blue uniform carrying a trombone. He looks to the right, then to the left, and seems extremely put out that there is absolutely no one around. He must have the wrong time or place.

I drink some water, sitting on a stool facing the window.

After a short time, weary from the landscape's monotony, I take from my pocket the paper on which Marcel wrote his phone numbers and the sentence *Bàbá tí mbi à kúì*. I try to sing it. I move quite easily from the low note to the two high notes but can't manage to get the middle tone. No doubt you have to leave a bigger gap between the other two. I start over, pitching my voice much lower, and then climbing very high. For a second I manage to find the middle level, but I lose it the next time I try. I take the liberty of associating the three tones with do, mi, and so. At least twenty times in a row I murmur do, so, so, mi. I have no trouble with the end of the sentence, *à kúì*—do, so, do. I give myself a little break and finish the bottle of water, then I do all the notes one by one: do, so, so, mi, do, so, do. I find the tune even sadder than before. It sounds like a farewell song.

Each time we move through a forest and the landscape darkens, I can make out on the window the face of the hostess, who is standing behind her little counter. Because she is blonde and her skin very white, her reflection is as pale as a specter. I order a cognac from her. Little by little I persuade myself that I have just lived through an exceptional day. When we get to Paris, I am almost convinced that the excursion I just took is but the beginning of a much longer journey.

As soon as I arrive, I sense that he is very tense. Is it because I'm five minutes late?

"It's very bad to be five minutes late for a meeting that has been planned so far ahead of time!" he says in the most disagreeable tone imaginable.

Immediately he begins poring over the menu, which he must know by heart since he comes to this restaurant so faithfully. Apparently his vacation didn't do him much good. He is pale with dark circles under his eyes, and only a slight sunburn on top of his head. He's wearing a navy blue short sleeve shirt and a pink tie that is loosened around his neck. He looks like a police detective in charge of a muddled, unimportant case.

"You should eat the cod brandade!" he says with the authority of a doctor prescribing medicine.

"Excellent idea!"

Is he disappointed by my reaction? He looks at me with stormy, mistrustful eyes. He's obviously trying to find an excuse to let his animosity run wild. But I'm too happy to see him to give him one. Will he wind up being angry with me because I refuse to share his wrath?

"I have something to tell you," I say.

Georges acts as if he didn't hear me and calls to the waitress, a middle-aged woman who comes limping over. He orders a bottle of wine, which is not at all usual for him. If he drinks wine in the state he's in, we'll end up in a fight before the meal is over.

The Japanese people talking at the table next to ours don't bother us. Because we don't understand a word they're saying, we hardly hear them. The handicapped waitress has a great deal of trouble holding the bowl of soup steady. She places it on the table with relief. Georges has ordered only this soup and smoked herring.

All the waitresses are middle-aged and seem very weary. It's as if they've been here since the very creation of the restaurant and are now dreaming of only one thing: that it will close forever. The establishment dates back to the late nineteenth century. There are still compartments for napkins that no longer serve any purpose, and baggage nets above the benches. No repairs or maintenance were ever done. Its revolving door sticks easily, its coat racks wobble the minute you touch them, its copper coat pegs are tarnished, and its mirror doesn't reflect much any more. It's the perfect place to meditate on the passing of time, and to relax. Its dilapidation allows you to let go. It is frequented by people who work in the neighborhood and by hip tourists. You have to admit that the food is tolerable and the prices are low. Georges only invites authors whom he considers friends here.

"Is your soup good?" I ask, just to break the silence.

"It's not hot enough."

Yet his bowl is steaming. Outside the sun is beating down. There's an ice cream vendor on every corner. I feel sorry for the cooks, whom I can see through a window cut out in the middle of the back wall. Because this window is rather low, I can only glimpse their hands passing the dishes to the waitresses. Most of them are black. Puffs of steam penetrate the room through this opening.

"Are you worried about something?"

I'm afraid of shocking him, he hates inquisitiveness. He's just as secretive as Alice. Still, he's not going to throw his soup in my face, is he? He finishes it deliberately, without batting an eyelid, lights a cigarillo and blows the smoke toward the French doors at the front of the restaurant, some of which are open.

"I have a daughter," he says.

He leaves me no time to show my surprise and continues speaking while watching the smoke disappear:

"She's twenty-eight now. She's Ethiopian, I adopted her five years ago. I met her when I was the Cultural Counselor in Addis Ababa, about twenty years ago. She had already lost her father at the time. Later I helped her come to Paris to study, and then I decided to adopt her. She has a lovely smile."

I feel so overwhelmed by this flood of revelations that I almost want to ask him to take a break. Won't he regret having told me all of it in the end? I didn't know he had been a Cultural Counselor, or that he had lived in Africa. Surely he'll approve of my project.

"Unfortunately, her mother is a shrew. She constantly claims she is about to die in order to keep her daughter from leaving again. She tries to get money out of me. The daughter doesn't fall for any of it, but, still, she feels sorry for her. She also has a brother who lives in Vitry-le-François, a little punk who already tried to confine his sister illegally. He also needs money. Jackie Santini is in Addis Ababa right now. He's going to try to reason with the mother and bring back the daughter."

So it was this brother's house that Jackie Santini was watching one night when it was fifteen degrees outside.

"I'm not in love with the girl. It would have been easier to marry her. The procedure for adopting an adult is much longer than the one for adopting a child, the county court let things drag on for two and a half years. But now I have a legal heir. I'm happy to know she'll inherit my books and the house in Trouville. Too bad if I can't see her more often. Our relations are as pure as those of Jean Valjean and Cosette!"

These secrets reveal someone I didn't know at all. They draw us closer together and at the same time push us further apart. How could I have thought for so long that his life consisted of nothing more than his work as a publisher? I certainly lacked insight. I never asked him why he had chosen to put Al Capone's picture up in his office. You can see the ocean and a boat on it, just as you can on the picture of Jules Verne. All of a sudden I feel very alone. The Japanese have left. The waitresses are gathered in front of the little window that leads to the kitchen and are chatting with the cooks. Georges is drawing some kind of mountain peaks on the paper tablecloth. They remind me of the cypress tree he felt moved to draw when my father died. It was surrounded by diagonal lines that represented rain. He must spend his days in Trouville painting seascapes. Is Ethiopia as flat as the Central African Republic? Jean met the Bourquins for the first time on Mount Cameroon. I would like to be able to convince myself that a link exists between all these faces that come into my mind, that they form a coherent whole. This would allow me to sleep peacefully for an hour or two. How much wine have I drunk? Georges has finished only one glass. Don Quixote manages to include in his dream every character he meets, every event he witnesses. He sleeps like a baby.

"I'll bet Santini went to Africa with his raincoat," I said.

"It's part of his character. It's a raincoat that doesn't come off. You should use Santini! He reminds me of some of your heroes. You could have invented him. If it's all right with you, I'll tell him when I call him that you're going to mention him in your next novel. It'll make him happy. He needs to be in a good mood to carry out the mission I entrusted him with. He was very jealous of the girl when he learned I had adopted her, he made a real scene. But now I think he likes her."

He spoke about his daughter in a quiet voice. Why had he written *pupulenge* in his notebook? Our lunch ends on a more agreeable note than the one on which it began. He orders two lemon tarts and two cups of coffee, without taking the trouble to consult me. The brandade was excellent. He didn't touch the smoked herring. When will I tell him the news I promised him? When the waitress brings over the coffee? Haven't I waited long enough?

"I'm thinking of going to Bangi, most likely next month."

I feel the same sense of relief I'd felt when I told Jean about my desire to learn an African language. It's harder to say things than to do them. I lean against the back of my chair and inhale deeply. To tell the truth, I feel completely out of breath, as if I had pronounced those words at the end of a very long race.

Georges says nothing. I recently discovered a travel agency in my neighborhood that sells tickets to Africa. It's been there for a long time, yet I'd never noticed it, any more than I'd noticed the elephant that symbolizes the sturdiness of my fridge. Will I really have the courage to go in one day and buy a ticket? It will require so much effort on my part that I'll probably collapse as soon as I've signed my check. I'll wake up in the travel agent's arms.

"Don't be afraid," she'll say to me, "the wildcats deserted Bangi ages ago. Only donkeys and domestic cats still roam the streets."

Paul-Marie Bourquin had taken a long time before getting up to take me into his library. I had become impatient. Georges remains impassive. He makes a sign to the waitress to speed it up. She's speeding it up as much as she can, poor dear. There's as much coffee in the saucers as there is in the cups she brings us. Georges savors his tart while taking little sips of coffee. And then he begins drawing again! He sketches out a few geometric figures and then begins a more convoluted drawing in which I soon see the outlines of Greece.

"Somehow I thought you would go to Greece," he said, "and that you would try to establish new bonds with your country. Don't you have anyone left there?"

"No one."

Mbi yeke gi mbi oko. He doesn't remember the shape of the Peloponnesus very well—it really has four points, not three.

"I understand, though, that you want to get to know Sango, to converse with the people in its family."

"I have the impression that it feels cramped in my apartment," I say. "Sango must wonder at times what it's doing here in Paris, in the home of a Greek."

"My daughter gives me the same impression when she comes to my house. She spends a lot of time looking out the window.... Is it an interesting language?"

He probably has a picture of his daughter in his wallet. In mine I put the piece of paper on which Marcel Alingbindo wrote. A pleasant tranquility encloses us. The few remaining customers are not talking much. The kitchen is closed: a shutter has been slid in front of the serving hatch. All the waitresses have left except one, the youngest, who is reading a newspaper at the edge of a table.

"Would you like another cup of coffee?" he asks.

He urges me to go see one of his friends who works for the Ministry of Foreign Affairs and is in charge of cultural exchange with African countries.

"She'll put you in touch with the French embassy and with its people in Africa. It's not a good idea to go to a country without knowing anyone. You'll need the French for the time it takes you to get set up and oriented. Santini also went to see this woman, her name is Mascaro, she's Corsican like he is. She'll probably ask you to give one or two lectures. She'll provide you with orders for a mission that will come in handy if you're stopped by the police or by soldiers."

"Do you think they might take me for a diamond thief?"

"Let me tell you, they don't fool around over there."

Suddenly I see myself surrounded by an angry mob armed with knives.

"After I have killed him, can I throw his corpse in the bush?" one of them asks.

Another suggests that they make me undergo the trial by poison. He must be the medicine man.

"If I drink the poison, I shall die," I protest.

Then I get the brilliant idea of showing them the picture of my grandfather taken in the Studio de Paris in Bangi.

"He's my grandfather!" I shout over them.

I realize that they don't understand French.

"*Baba ti baba ti mbi!*" I tell them, handing them the photograph, which they examine in amazement.

They wonder what course of action to take. A French *coopérant* tugs at my sleeve and exhorts me to flee.

"*Mbi ye Beafrika!*" I continue enthusiastically. "*Mbi yeke nzoni na kodoro ti ala! Beafrika a nzere na le ti mbi!*"

"What are you saying?" the *coopérant* asks me.

"I'm telling them that I love Central Africa, that I am happy in their county, that Central Africa is pleasing to my eyes!"

I see Marcel Alingbindo's smile spread across each of their faces.

"Check with the Greek authorities to find out if they have a delegation in Bangi," Georges insists. "Whom are you going to call if you fall ill? If I were you, I'd go to the Pasteur Institute right away. Some of the vaccinations you'll need can't be given in one time, you'll have to wait two weeks or a month for the booster. Buy some syringes before you leave, don't ever let yourself get a shot with the ones they use in their hospitals."

"But I'm not going to fall ill!"

He rejects my optimism. He probably thinks I'm too relaxed for someone who is contemplating going to Africa.

"Well, I warned you."

His voice takes on the surly tone it had an hour ago. The waitress doesn't seem in a hurry to see us leave. She lives too far away to go home when the restaurant closes.... She sleeps there on a bench.... She hasn't been home in years.... She'll never know if she's been robbed.

"If I were more worried, I wouldn't go," I say. "Maybe I'm not worried enough because I don't really believe in my project. I don't know why I made this decision."

"Anyone can make a decision without knowing why and still be sure it is the right one," he says calmly.

"All right then, tomorrow I'll go to the Pasteur Institute."

I tell him about my visit with Marcel, about his efforts to preserve and enrich Sango.

"I didn't know it was possible to love a language so much."

I explain to him that since Sango doesn't have a word for "snow," Snow White would be translated as "Dust from the Cold."

"That would make a nice title."

Naturally he's read Etienne Goyémidé's *The Silence of the Forest.*

"The author must have lived among the Pygmies. He makes them seem very sympathetic, without ever overdoing it. He tries to restore them to favor because they are often scorned by other Africans, probably because they are so small."

I tell him that Marcel and his family said a prayer for God to help me with my work on Sango. He becomes thoughtful.

"You can't get out of it now.... You have to see your work through. One day you'll leave Sango behind. You're not thinking of moving to Africa permanently, are you? Can you imagine how Dumas would have recounted the prayer scene if he had been in your shoes? The marvelous words he would have found to express his surprise and his emotion? He could have written thirty pages about it!"

I can't imagine it. I've no talent for lyrical flights. I'm happy just to record events that I don't understand.

I haven't opened my Sango books in quite a while. Very early one morning I went to the Pasteur Institute. The waiting room was already full. I spent two good hours there, contemplating the receptionist's legs, scrutinizing faces, examining the map of world health. Each epidemic is represented by a different color. I felt a touch of anxiety when I saw that the Central African Republic was one of the most colorful countries. I went outside to smoke my pipe. This allowed me to pull myself together and to go back to my seat.

There were African women accompanied by their children, Arabs getting ready to go to Mecca, a nun with a waxen face who was reading Romain Gary's *Roots of Heaven*—I saw an exhausted elephant on the cover, which reminded me of the sentence *adoli a kui*—and smiling young men. Their happy-go-lucky attitude annoyed me, just as mine had annoyed Georges. There were middle-aged Frenchmen dressed like the adventurers one sees on television, in wide trousers and multi-pocketed, waterproofed vests. They looked like they had just returned from Africa, for they were very tan. They put on important airs and were constantly looking up, as if they were bird watching. Great travelers are not necessarily the most agreeable people.

"Do you get many tourists to Central Africa?" I asked the nurse.

Her answer was music to my ears: "Very few."

She was in such a hurry to get to the next person that I wasn't surprised by the abruptness of her answer. She injected me with four vaccinations, prescribed pills to take before and during my trip, and gave me an appointment a month later for the booster shot about which Georges had warned me.

I left the Institute, relieved that I had overcome this obstacle. On the way home, I realized I was looking at the city in a strange and amused way, as if I had been gone a long time and were in the process of discovering it anew. It was only once I got home that I started to feel ill. By evening I was flat on my back. The nurse had mentioned that the hepatitis B vaccination might give me a fever. I spent the next day in bed, watching the colors of epidemics twirl around as if in a kaleidoscope and wondering if I would survive my journey. The possibility of dying in the Central African Republic seemed less painful to me when I considered that my great aunt Clotilde Bérémian's family must have a vault ready to accept me in the Bangi cemetery. These sad thoughts were only interrupted by the barking of the dog that my concierge had recently acquired. The animal was in the courtyard. Sometimes his curiosity would lead him to the building entrance. He's a huge black monster, and I avoid him like the plague. I told myself that I should conquer the terror his fangs inspire in me and get used to facing him calmly. I would meet much more fearsome animals in the jungle. In addition to the barking, I could hear trumpeting, roaring, and an incredible variety of birdcalls. I regretted that there were no spiders on my ceiling with whom I could learn to live in symbiosis.

The next day, having more or less regained my strength, I went to see Marie-Ange Mascaro, an imposing woman of about sixty who received me in a cramped office on the fourth floor of the Ministry of Foreign Affairs. Among the maps spread out on the walls, I spotted the one of the Central African Republic that I had at home. Our conversation began in the best possible way: she told me she had read all my books. She hadn't bought them—"Georges sends me everything he publishes," she told me—but at least she had read them.

"Even *Monk Gaspard's Three Sisters*?"

"Oh, no, not that one!"

She confessed her preference for *Letter to Marika*.

"Was that really your mother's name?"

A very distant image of my mother surreptitiously appeared to me. I saw her in the shop, seated in front of her sewing machine. She had an expression of concentration, of worry almost, on her face. The daylight, made softer by the glass roof, enveloped her completely. She was working in a golden cloud.

"Isn't it difficult to write in French?"

While she was speaking to me, she was looking for something in the documents piled on her desk. There were so many and they were stacked so high that they formed a kind of modern city. Her violet lighter made me think of a futurist car and her pack of menthol cigarettes, which was green, of a small park.

"The problems I face when I write in Greek console me for the ones I face in French."

She finally extricated a sheet of paper and held it out to me. I realized then that she was extremely efficient, for the page was entitled "Mr. Nicolaides' Trip to Bangui."

"I've already informed Yves Bidou, our Cultural Counselor, about your visit. Together we set up your timetable. I explained to him that you were learning Sango and that you would especially like to meet Africans."

The note I was looking at indeed indicated that a meeting with Central African writers, another meeting with students from the Boganda quarter, and a conference at the library of the French Cultural Center were planned for me. The more I read, the harder it was for me to convince myself that all this had to do with me, that I wasn't reading an excerpt from a novel. On what page did I come in? Despite my confusion, I was charmed by the idea of meeting fellow writers and even more enchanted by the thought of meeting students. At the bottom of the page were the addresses of Yves Bidou and Sammy Mbo-lieada, the president of the Writers Club, both of whom lived in Bangi.

"Is this acceptable to you?"

I had a slight nervous twitch when I saw her take up the telephone receiver.

"Whom are you calling?"

"Yves!"

Yves answered immediately. She told him that I had agreed to host the three events and promised to send him my most recent books via diplomatic pouch. Then she gave the phone to me. Suddenly I was fed up with all my anxiety and reticence, and I decided to rise to the occasion.

"So, Yves, how's it going?" I asked, as if we were friends.

He assured me that he would do everything in his power to facilitate my stay. He would place independent housing that belonged to the French Embassy at my disposal.

"Everyone here is eager to welcome you. We have so few visitors! Bangi doesn't attract many people anymore."

I had glued the receiver to my ear in order to pick up all the sounds, the pounding of a torrential downpour, the cry of an animal or a bird.

"Is there a particular site that you'd like to visit?"

The opportunity to show my knowledge was too good to pass up.

"Sorcerers' Lake!" I answered with assurance.

"All right, I'll see what I can do.... When are you coming?"

I recalled my appointment at the Pasteur Institute.

"In a little more than a month."

"Yes, it will be better if you come after the September 19 presidential elections. The atmosphere will be less tense."

"He's a delightful man," said Marie-Ange shortly afterwards.

"And very cultured. You'll recognize him easily at the airport, he looks like Louis de Funès."

All this fuss around me started to make me suspicious. What exactly was expected of me? My eyes were drawn from time to time to a huge directory of the Francophone world that was lying on a shelf. "They're not interested in my books but in the fact that I have written a few of them in French." For a moment I saw Marie-Ange more as a representative of the Ministry of Foreign Affairs than as a friend of Georges's.

"You know that young Central Africans are still not allowed to study their mother tongue in school? They get the same education they did before independence, and it tends to strip them of their culture. It would be extremely painful for me to write in French if I had to give up Greek. I can praise the study of languages, not the forgetting of them."

Her response made me realize that she had many fine qualities in addition to her efficiency and her enthusiasm. In fact, she took her time before answering me. For quite a while she gazed out the window on a garden where two stone benches sat facing one another. A white cat was sprawled out on one of them. "It's Mathilde's cat," I thought.

"My mother tongue is Corsican, but I never studied it seriously," she said at last. "And I regret it deeply. Now I can only say a couple of things in Corsican. Languages that aren't taught become stupid. The French State's crusade against Corsican and Occitan, which has been going on since 1880, seems ridiculous to me. I think my compatriots would have become much better French citizens if France had respected their culture. Would it be indiscreet to ask you why you are studying Sango?"

"I don't know.... I find it hard to believe that anyone would ever regret having learned any language."

Once we had had this discussion, I would have been completely at ease with my project and almost ready to leave if there hadn't been one point that still needed clarification. While I congratulated myself for having chosen a country neglected by tourists, I wanted to know why it had been thus abandoned.

"I meant to speak to you about this. There is only one flight a week to Bangi, and it is overrun with employees of the oil companies in Chad because its first stop is N'Djamena. The Central African Republic has no oil. Flights leaving from Bangi are often cancelled for lack of fuel. It's difficult to get there, difficult to leave, and even more difficult to stay. The people are not very fond of the French, who left a bad taste in the mouths of the Central Africans, and their aid in repressing the 1996 and 1997 rebellions against Patassé did nothing to help their reputation."

"France is supporting Patassé?"

She was quiet again. Was she sorting through the information that she was able to give me? It seemed, rather, as though she were puzzled.

"France supports him from a distance, while looking the other way. It provides considerable aid to Central Africa but does not want to receive Patassé in Paris. It withdrew its troops last year and has greatly reduced the number of aid workers it sends there. Patassé distrusts the French, just as he distrusts everyone. He has so little faith in his own army that his presidential palace is guarded by Libyan soldiers. He will most likely win the elections in September. The opposition is divided, and of course in Africa it is always the men already in power who win the elections. And did I mention that the economic situation is a shambles? Civil servants have not been paid for a year and they refuse to work. Forty-eight percent of the population lives on less than one hundred francs a month."

A few of the quotations I had read in the dictionary flashed through my mind: "I shall die from misery," "He is dressed in rags," "I don't even have enough money to buy salt." The picture she was painting was so bleak that the presence of Louis de Funès's twin seemed perfectly incongruous to me.

"In spite of all this, it is a very endearing country. I was there last month. If I had the feeling that it was at all risky for you, I would forbid you to go. Do you still want to?"

"I do."

I had no trouble at all saying those words. They were, in fact, simply an echo of the "I do" I had answered when Paul-Marie Bourquin had asked me if I really wanted to learn Sango. "Finally I will be able to hear this language."

Marie-Ange was overjoyed by my answer. She offered to take care of my visa. "Just bring me your passport about ten days before you're ready to leave."

She was in the mood to joke: "I see that you are much less sensitive to the cold than Santini!"

I wasn't wearing a raincoat, of course.

Later that afternoon I sent her an affectionately dedicated copy of *Monk Gaspard's Three Sisters*. And then I took care of my ticket. I crossed the threshold of my neighborhood travel agency with confidence. I didn't feel the need to snuggle up in the arms of the secretary who made my reservation. We set my departure date for Saturday, October 2, and the return two weeks later. The plane was to leave at 11:00 PM.

"You'll get into Bangi Sunday morning."

So I would hear the church bells ringing when I got off the plane.

Then I went to my friend Nondas's, on the rue de l'Échelle, to get another plane ticket, to Athens.

Putting my parents' house up for sale took much longer than I thought. I had to use a lawyer and collect countless certificates and affidavits. I paid the taxes that my father owed for the first part of the year, when he was still alive. The weather was beautiful during the two weeks I spent in Athens, yet every morning when I awoke I thought I heard rain.

I went only once to my parents' house, on a Saturday. I had rented a van. In the end, I took away quite a few things: my father's armchair, a painting the town council had given him for his fiftieth birthday, his Thermos, my mother's little electric sewing machine, the tea service that reminded me of the evenings I'd spent alone with her. Rummaging through the wardrobe, where there were now only my father's clothes, I was thrilled to find the dress she had created for the character of Mary Stuart—a magnificent white dress fitted at the waist, with panniers, puffed sleeves, and a stiff collar. While I was wrapping it in plastic, I remembered the note from the play's director. It had said that Schiller liked to smell the odor of rotten pears while he was writing and he kept several in one of his desk drawers.

The wardrobe also held a cardboard box filled with letters from various women. I set them on fire in the back of the yard. They took a long time to burn. An hour later all that remained among the ashes was the corner of a page with two words on it: "Dear Yannis." I kept that little piece of paper.

When I had finished putting all those things into the van, as well as three crates I had filled with various papers, I invited the women I knew in the neighborhood to come take the rest. Some came with their husbands, others with their children. The Bulgarian woman arrived escorted by three strapping fellows. She was angry to find other people there, deeming that all these things belonged to her as a matter of course, given the role she had played in my father's life. I gave her money to calm her down, but I refused to give up the Marie Stuart dress, the existence of which she was fully aware.

I offered coffee to everyone, just as I had done on March 7. Mrs. Voula cried when she spoke to me about my parents. She confessed that she had liked my mother more than my father.

"Marika was a remarkable woman," she said to me.

When the day was over, the house was empty. Only a chair remained. I went upstairs to make sure nothing had been forgotten. Even the cleaning products had disappeared from the bathroom. When I walked down the steps, I avoided the stair that creaked, as if the sound could still wake my parents.

I didn't have the heart to close the shutters. I took leave of the garden by looking at the trees, one at a time. The lemon tree returned my farewell by offering me a beautiful fruit, which I put in my pocket.

Stanislas was in the warehouse behind city hall that was used as a workshop and storage area. He was yelling at a worker who had come to deliver half a dozen caskets. Lined up flat on the ground, the crates gave off a strong smell of resin. Stanislas grabbed one, stood it up, and kicked it hard on its lid. When it hit the ground, it fell to pieces.

"Tell your boss to get over here," he said.

The worker didn't utter another word. Stanislas is a giant. He is over six feet six and fearsomely strong, despite the fact that he is seventy years old and as skinny as a rail. My father used to tell me that he scared the families, who viewed him as a reincarnation of Charon.

He calmed down when he saw me. He placed his huge hands on my shoulders and shook me vigorously, as if wanting to make sure that my legs wouldn't give way beneath me.

We went to the cemetery on foot. He walked quickly with his head bowed, indifferent to the hustle and bustle of the streets. He told me that he wanted to offer me an icon as a gift. I thought of the very beautiful one he had painted for my father, which I had placed in the casket the day he was buried.

"Would you like that?"

He knew I didn't share his faith. He thought his icon would insidiously make me change my mind.

My plan to visit Africa seemed absolutely insane to him.

"You don't want to go there!" he exclaimed, horrified.

Perhaps he could already picture me in the cauldron of a tribe of cannibals?

"I'm sure Mr. Yannis would have advised you against such a journey!"

He had always kept a certain respectful distance from my father, despite their friendship. I never heard Stanislas call him by just his first name.

We fell silent when we got to the gates of the cemetery. We took the path to plot 323, zigzagging among the monuments just as I had as a child playing with the ball.

"Did you see the flowers?" he asked me when we had stopped.

They were dazzling. They had grown so much that they hid the edges of the marble slab.

"I water them every morning.... I come to see my friend."

I didn't want to cry. "I'll cry another time, another day.... I'll cry in Africa." We didn't stay long in front of the tomb. And yet I had time to imagine that a little boy would one day learn to read by spelling the names of my parents, Marika and Yannis Nicolaides, inscribed in gold letters on the stone.

"I couldn't do this job if I didn't believe," Stanislas murmured.

We went back to city hall because I needed one more paper to complete the list my lawyer had drawn up. Stanislas's son, who had taken over from my father, had gone to lunch with the secretary. Brand new crescent-shaped desks, equipped with computers, had replaced the old ones. In the back room, though, where I had drawn as a child, nothing had changed. The braid of garlic was still hanging behind the door.

"I found the subject of the icon that I'm going to make. It will represent Saint George slaying the dragon! He is the destroyer of the most hateful animals, serpents in particular. When one wants to drive serpents out of a region, one always calls on him!"

A week later he indeed brought it to my house. It's no bigger than a paperback. Orange flames shoot out of the dragon's mouth. Stanislas insists that I carry it with me during my journey.

What will happen to my things when I die? Who will open my files, my drawers, my wardrobe? Who will take possession of my apartment? Must I adopt a young Ethiopian woman to take this load off my mind?

I tried as best as I could to avoid questions. I didn't attempt to figure out how my parents' disappearance would affect the direction my life would take. I was content to see that the streets looked as they always had. It wasn't very pleasant for me to hear Greek spoken around me. The words hurt. At times they made me want to put my hands over my ears. I felt that my mother tongue had betrayed me.

I saw only a few friends and Antigone, my publisher. She is going to publish *The Tin Soldier* in December, the least propitious month for selling novels. She'll need me to be here to launch the book. I realized that it was impossible for me to think about the future. My thoughts stopped at the threshold of Africa and refused to go any further. In front of me an impassable forest loomed.

Yorgos was the only one who thoroughly approved of my project. He swore he would have gladly accompanied me if he could have closed his ad agency. He recalled the adventures of Gaour and Tarzan even better than I did: he told me that Tatabou's father was the chief of a tribe descended from Alexander the Great! He reminded me that Gaour had a mischievous friend, a Pygmy, whose name was Pocopico.

He asked me to say hello to Tarzan for him. "Tell him that he has friends in Greece, in spite of his ill will toward Gaour."

The Greek consulate in Bangi has been closed for a long time, and its archives have vanished. There are only a handful of Greeks who remain in the Central African Republic. I obtained this information from a civil servant in the Office of Emigration of the Ministry of Foreign Affairs.

The name of my mother's cousin who lived in Cape Town was Leander.

"Did you know that the first big hotel in Bangi was built by a certain André Panayotopoulos? Another of our compatriots, whose name was Psimis, was once appointed minister of education by Bokassa. But it seems that he didn't speak our language. His father was Greek and his mother was African."

I noted these details with pleasure. I thought they were a good omen for my stay. Psimis must have been as dark as Gaour.

"No one chased the Greeks out of Bangi. They merely got old without finding anyone to replace them, because on the one hand Africa lost the appeal it once had and on the other Greeks no longer wanted to leave their own country. The mass exodus has stopped!"

He told me this in a conceited tone, as if he had personally contributed to this happy turn of affairs.

"You'll see that most of the shops now belong to Lebanese, and to a few Portuguese as well. If by any chance you were to hear something about the archives of our consulate, would you be so kind as to let me know?"

I am trying to make the final preparations for my departure calmly. Whenever I feel my courage flagging, I look at the photo of my grandfather that I temporarily placed on the bookshelf in front of the *Grand Robert*. I imagine the dangers to which he had to expose himself to get from Alexandria to Bangi in 1911. The rifle he is holding is not a toy.

So I force myself to show a sangfroid worthy of this courageous ancestor, but it's not always easy. Georges talked to me for over half an hour on the phone about the ravages caused by mosquitoes and advised me to get my hands on a variety of products, pomades, lotions, as well as a ton of ultrasonic mosquito repellants and a mosquito net. He didn't mention tsetse flies. He probably thinks their feats are so well known that I need not be reminded of them.

Jean cautioned me about AIDS, which affects fifteen percent of the Central African Republic's population, and about the sun.

"You cannot imagine the size of the sun in the tropics," he told me. "It practically fills the whole sky!"

He urged me to buy condoms, a hat, sunglasses. According to Alice, I'll also need a cell phone. She gave me a present, a compass that looks like a huge watch. She's convinced that it's easy to get lost in Africa. But isn't that why one goes there?

Since I returned from Greece, there have been more and more television shows about great predators. On Channel 5, there is a movie about pythons; "Planet" is interested in *The Legend of the Lion*; Channel 6 is broadcasting a program in two parts called *Those Animals that Kill* (the first part is on crocodiles, the second on big cats), and on Arte, the cultural channel, which usually doesn't set much store by animals, there will be a show called *The Adventurer and the Cayman* on the Friday before I leave. Channel 1 is offering, at the same time, something called *Anaconda*, a fictional movie starring a giant snake. I know that this reptile thrives in South America, but how do I know it doesn't have relatives in Bangi? Alas, *Tarzan the Apeman* with Johnny Weissmuller, which I would have loved to see again, is not scheduled on any channel.

The news on television is not reassuring either. There are reports on the violent battles now taking place in the Democratic Republic of the Congo between the partisans of President Laurent-Désiré Kabila and the members of the National Council for the Defense of Democracy-Forces for the Defense of Democracy. The conflict risks throwing the whole region into unrest because the dictatorship set up by Kabila is relying on Zimbabwean and Angolan armed forces, whereas the resistance is supported by Uganda and Rwanda, which have already invaded the eastern portion of the country. What are the Central Africans doing in all this? Are they content merely to observe the events taking place on the opposite bank of the Ubangi? Does the river constitute a sufficient barrier against the warring factions? Is it wide enough to foil stray bullets? Must I include a rifle among the items I need to buy?

I am too preoccupied to return to a serious study of Sango. I simply learned the phrases "greetings," *mbi bara mo* (literally, "I greet you"), "how is it going?" *tongana nye?* (literally, "how what?"), and "thank you very much," *singila mingi.*

123

Sometimes I become aware of an immense hush, as if the entire city had become silent. Is this the silence that precedes great cataclysms? I'm not so sure. Examining yet again the map of Africa in the *Larousse*, I discovered that the Central African Republic is located on the same meridian as Greece. I also learned that it is in the same time zone as Paris. In other words, I'm not going very far.

5

I was pleasantly surprised to see that my arrival in Bangi had drawn a small crowd; I'm not used to having people wait for me in airports. About twenty porters raced over to me, their eyes riveted on my lone suitcase. The first discussion I heard in Sango was an altercation among these porters. I didn't grasp a single word of what they said. Was this because I was dazed? Because they were screaming? Anger deforms languages, it makes them unrecognizable. I was very concerned with the fate of my bag as I watched it going off first in one direction, then in another. One man would hoist it up with great difficulty, another would pull it energetically across the floor as if it were a stubborn animal.

The last man to grab it was Yves Bidou, who ended the melee by distributing a few coins. Indeed, he does resemble Louis de Funès, but his affable smile and his calm air are his and his alone. In addition, he is much more robust than the comedian. Dozens of women, children, and old people were waiting for the few black passengers arriving from Paris.

We climbed into a Japanese four-wheel drive, but we didn't get far. Another group, made up of soldiers and policemen, was lying in wait for us at the parking lot exit. They didn't look like they were fooling around. I thought that already the time had come for me to show my mission orders. They examined the vehicle's registration for a long while. At first, I felt as though I were still in Paris, far from these characters in uniform, some of whom had their noses pushed up against the car windows. Then, all of a sudden, I realized that I had arrived. This awareness roused me completely and made me feel almost intoxicated. I needed to speak. So I rolled down my window, something Bidou had strictly forbidden me to do, and addressed the oldest policeman, who was wiping his neck with a handkerchief.

I said, "*Mbi bara mo. Tongana nye?*"

He drew closer and gave me a long answer that remained utterly impenetrable for me. He seemed enchanted. His colleagues were watching the scene with curiosity. Yves Bidou again proceeded to dole out money. Shortly afterward, the barrier was raised.

"*Singila mingi!*" I cried to the old policeman, who responded with a friendly wave of the hand.

Finally we were on the road to Bangi. It was a saffron-colored trail barely suitable for cars, with huge bumps and holes as deep as graves. I was literally so shaken that I could hear the coins rattling in my pockets. Frequently Yves had to veer off the trail in order go forward. I offered to reimburse him for the tips he had given out at the airport. He firmly refused my offer.

"I'm used to paying. You're in a country that is badly in need of money. Even the policemen are thinking of going on strike. They haven't gotten a cent since June 1998. And then, I believe we owe the Central Africans something: we lived in their country for seventy years without ever having paid them the slightest rent. The city of Bangi was founded in 1889 by French soldiers."

The condition of the road made it impossible to have a sustained conversation. He drove carefully, muttering a few words from time to time. The bumps and jolts didn't bother me in the least. I considered them part of a new game. I was as happy as a child at a county fair.

Here and there along the path tall trees were planted a good distance from one another, in single file. Their lower branches were so far from the ground that even Tarzan would have had difficulty reaching them. They shaded modest adobe huts covered with straw or palm leaves. Yves informed me that the trees were mango trees and the orangey color of the landscape was caused by laterite dust.

A lot of people were walking toward the city on either side of the road. We were driving in the middle of a double procession. It was just as I had read in the dictionary: the people were balancing heavy loads on their heads—wide baskets full of fruit, bags of manioc or coal, wooden beams—and this made them a great deal taller. A young man was transporting a crate filled with live chickens, and they appeared to be in top form. On their backs, most of the women were also carrying babies wrapped in fabric, the tips tied around their chests or foreheads. Yet our traveling companions went forward smoothly, swinging their arms as if their burdens were light. We drove past a bustling market.

"We are at Kilometer 5," Yves told me. "Places are often named according to their distance in kilometers from the center of Bangi. It's a custom inherited from the city's military past."

We passed a taxi. It was the same yellow as the taxis in Athens, and it was packed. In Athens, too, taxis accept several passengers at once. I was so convinced I had penetrated another world that its least exotic aspects were also striking. Most of the men and half the women were dressed like Europeans. Some were carrying only a briefcase or a purse. Many had cell phones. A man was peacefully speaking into his phone beneath a mountain of green bananas that covered half his face. He was probably taking an order. It was cloudy, like in Paris, and it couldn't have been more than twenty degrees Celsius.

I noticed an unremarkable, three-story building made of cement. A hundred meters farther, Yves shut off the engine and motioned me to get out of the car.

"We are in the city center," he assured me emphatically, as if to banish any doubts I might have had.

With the exception of the three-story building, no other structure emerged from the crowd that surrounded us, crushed us, hindered us from moving ahead. Where on earth did all these people live? Was Bangi hidden by their merchandise and their parasols? I was tempted to climb up on Bidou's broad shoulders to convince myself that there was indeed a city around us.

Struggling to move ahead, we managed to arrive at a Lebanese pastry shop called Phoenicia located on a street corner. It had a miniscule terrace that was relatively calm because a wire fence protected it from the mass of pedestrians. It resembled a chicken coop. I immediately spotted the three flies that were lazing about on our table. Did they belong to the same species as those infamous insects that had decimated the Arab cavalry? Yves paid them no mind. And in fact they seemed no more ferocious than their Greek cousins. A black customer was reading his newspaper while a child shined his shoes. We ordered coffee from the waitress, a slender girl with thick lips. She had put lipstick only on her upper lip. "Clotilde used to come drink her coffee here.... Back then, the establishment belonged to Greeks."

"I don't really feel like I'm in the center of a city," I acknowledged. "It's more like a distant suburb."

"It's true that you can't see any buildings from here. There are very few, in any case. And yet Bangi is a big city. It spreads over more than twelve kilometers and has half a million inhabitants. But it is not built upward, it is a labyrinth of small huts. Even though it is a hundred years old, it's still the size of a child. It's a child lost in the crowd."

The wire fence served mainly to keep beggars out. Several characters in rags laid siege to the terrace. Some of them were dragging themselves across the ground because they had lost their legs. They edged forward by pushing themselves with their hands. They used their espadrilles so as not to injure them: they were wearing the espadrilles on their hands. From time to time a cop would attempt to disperse them.

"Your apartment is in the residential quarter on the hill, twenty minutes from here on foot. You won't be far from the French embassy."

Wealthy Athenians also live on a hill, Lycabettus Hill.

"Does the hill have a name?"

"Not to my knowledge. They say that it was home to a lot of panthers in the past, but there aren't any now."

The flies left the table only when the girl brought the coffee.

"*Singila mingi*," I said to her, but she didn't hear me.

On occasion the clamor of the crowd became deafening. It was as if the inhabitants of Bangi hadn't seen each other for years and had a lot of news to tell each other, an enormous amount of business to attend to. The coffee was slightly bitter, yet I drank it with great pleasure, as if the city itself were offering it to me. Little by little I began to feel the same euphoria I had experienced coming out of the airport.

Our neighbor's newspaper was smaller than a tabloid and had very few pages. It was written in French, but its title was a Greek word: *Democrat*. The front page had these headlines across it:

ELECTORAL COUP D'ÉTAT IN CENTRAL AFRICA:
CHIRAC AND BONGO PLAY THE PATASSÉ CARD.
PATASSÉ ELECTED IN THE FIRST ROUND:
AN INTERNATIONAL PLOT HATCHED AGAINST
THE CENTRAL AFRICAN PEOPLE.

"Have you ever read Romain Gary's *The Roots of Heaven?*"

Yves' question frustrated me. I would have preferred to ask him about the political situation. I remembered the nun who was reading the book in the waiting room at the Pasteur Institute.

"Is it a good novel?"

He wore the same doubtful expression I had seen on Marie-Ange Mascaro when I questioned her about France's attitude toward Patassé. "It's a face they learn to make in the Ministry of Foreign Affairs; it's taught to them by an old, retired ambassador."

"Gary pleads brilliantly for the protection of elephants. In fact he expresses two views, one in favor of the elephants and the other against the pro-Soviet separatist movements. His anticommunism is more sincere than his love of animals... Are you interested in politics?"

"Not really. Small events engage me more than large ones, perhaps because they seem more accessible. Still, I'd like to know your thoughts about the elections that just took place."

"There's not much to say about them. Patassé was reelected with fifty-one percent of the vote. The opposition requested that the vote be invalidated, denouncing the registration of phony voters in the Northern conscriptions, which favor the incumbent powers. The constitutional court just ruled against it."

He skimmed the headlines of the paper that had been left on the table. Our neighbor had gotten up to greet a young woman. He touched the woman's forehead three times with his own, two on the right, one on the left, in precisely the same way that Yvonne Alingbindo had said goodbye to me. I felt a keen emotion on seeing this woman. Of course she didn't have Tatabou's thick and wavy mane — she had thin braids plastered to her head — but she had Tatabou's breasts. She was wearing only a tee shirt that was as wispy as gossamer. Yves Bidou paid her no mind.

"Omar Bongo, the President of Gabon and the senior Head of State in Central Africa, has been criticized for his role in convincing the opposition leaders to accept Patassé's victory, and Chirac has been reproached for having sent three thousand troops to Libreville to dissuade the people from protesting in the streets. But the leaders in question are washed up ex-presidents and former prime ministers in whom the people no longer believe."

I was listening to him but thinking about the young woman. She was speaking Sango with her friend. I didn't want to betray my feelings. I was content to observe her shadow on the cement flooring. I reviewed the sentences that I would have liked to say to her: *Mo nzere na le ti mbi*, "you are pleasing to my eyes," *Be ti mbi a yeke na mo*, "my heart is for you," *Mbi ye mo mingi*, "I love you very much."

"Besides, they have the same tribal chief mentality as Patassé. They are concerned solely with the interests of their own ethnic group. The unity of the country is fragile."

A young disabled man stopped in front of the wire fencing and stared at each customer, one at a time, before going on his way. He could only stand with the help of his two crutches. He walked like a puppet with dislocated limbs.

"Doesn't the fact that people haven't been paid for so long cause them problems?"

"They all grow manioc, corn, and yams on the outskirts of the city. Fortunately, nature is generous. It provides them with fruit, cooking oils, wine, fish, meat, and wood with which to build fires. They make pictures with butterfly wings, which they sell to foreigners. And from time to time they protest. Union officials are in the process of replacing politicians."

The road that leads to the hill goes along the central market, a large building surrounded by wooden stalls and peddlers, then passes by police headquarters and the presidential residence, invisible behind a high wall, comes across a quadrangular pedestal upon which a statue of Jean-Bedel Bokassa once sat, crosses through a small square still named after Valéry Giscard d'Estaing, the ex-emperor's good friend, and is swallowed up by a cluster of tall trees much denser than the one on Lycabettus Hill. There are indeed a few colonial houses, recognizable from the outsized roofs that protect the veranda as well, but there are so few of them that one wonders why the panthers bothered to leave.

The apartment reserved for me is a duplex, the first in a long, narrow structure with three other, identical apartments. The last is set aside for a film production company financed by the European Union; the middle ones are empty. Samba, the guardian, lives in a hut at the back of the yard. He opens the double gate at the property's entrance for us. He's a small man with powerful legs, a jovial expression, and a sharp eye.

At first I had the impression of penetrating a prison. The door to my apartment is reinforced and the windows have fat bars across them; they are also equipped with screens to keep out the mosquitoes. What struck me the most, though, was how much it resembled my parent's house. I found the same living room and the same kitchen on the ground floor, the same bedrooms separated from each other by the bathroom on the second floor. As for the stairway, it is identical to the one in Athens. Obviously I put my weight on the second to last one going up, but it didn't creak. I recalled thinking of my parents' stairs when I was at Marcel Alingbindo's.

"Is it all right?" Yves asked me as I was examining the bedroom.

The furniture was nothing out of the ordinary, yet I was happy to find a small table in front of the window. I even rushed to place on it the book with the blue binding in which I take notes, W. J. Reed's textbook, and the dictionary. A large tree concealed part of the landscape. Was it another mango tree? I could see a part of the garden, the outer wall crowned with shards of bottle glass, and the forest that began at the edge of the path we had taken.

"I have no passion for politics either, really."

He was kind enough to lend me a cell phone and to change some money for me. I made him out a check for four thousand francs, the amount I thought I would spend during my stay. He gave me back a huge packet of CFA francs. I was in a hurry for him to leave, and a bit frightened as well. I wondered how I would live through my first moments of solitude in Bangi.

"Shall I come back to get you around eight tonight?"

He had planned a dinner with Sammy Mbolieda, and perhaps with another *coopérant*, the librarian at the French Cultural Center.

I sat down on the corner of the bed when he left. My mood faltered. I reacted by getting up to search for an ashtray. I found one in the kitchen. There was only a bottle of water in the refrigerator, which was making so much noise it sounded like it was about to take off. Samba had lit a fire outside and was warming up a pot that he held by its handle. I thought about the little pile of letters burned in the garden in Athens. I opened the window.

"May I ask you a question?" I said to him, using the formal *vous*.

He came toward me, still carrying his pot where palm nuts were simmering.

"You have to say *tu* to me, boss!" he scolded me.

He was much younger than I.

"Okay. Do you understand this sentence: *Baba ti mbi a ye giriri apupulenge mingi?*"

"Your father used to love girls! You speak Sango!"

"Yes, Samba, I speak it but, alas, I don't understand it! How do you say 'Stay well'?

"One really says, 'leave well,' *gue nzoni.*"

"*Singila mingi.*"

This little bit of conversation cheered me immensely. I took a shower without putting my things away—I thought I had already wasted enough time in my life putting things away—and I went out with the dictionary under my arm.

When you have four posts a meter and a half to two meters long, and a few planks and cardboard boxes, you usually don't think of yourself as a homeowner. And yet you are. Along the streets of Bangi, several families, thousands of families no doubt, live in these basic shelters. A piece of cloth or a tarp serves as a front wall. These are houses where only small dreams can be dreamt. They are mere dormitories. Their occupants really live outside. They wash in the street, cook in the street, eat in the street. The street is a kind of inner courtyard. It's not unusual to come across tables and chairs, toys fabricated from steel wire, large cooking pots filled with a milky gruel, lamb grilling on a wood fire, and chickens running around freely. The tables and chairs are low to the ground, as if the city were inhabited by midgets. I realized the stool that Clotilde had brought me was not, as I had believed at the time, a child's seat.

There are countless fires burning, one in front of each shelter, approximately every five meters. The city gives off a smell that at first catches you unawares. It's the smell of food cooking and of burned wood. It's also not unusual to come across a sewing machine—I found the same machines in Bangi as the ones in the shop where my mother worked—a butcher's block, or a hairdresser's chair. People also work in the street. There are no shops, but there are signs nailed to the trees, written in French: "SALON DE COIFFEUR," "MODES DE PARIS." The hairdressers' signs are illustrated with drawings representing various haircuts, each with a number. This way, there are no misunderstandings with the customers, and conversations are kept to a minimum. Local hairdressers are apparently less talkative than their Greek counterparts. Bangi lets you realize that walls are not as indispensable to life as you think when you are in cities like Athens or Paris.

Behind these makeshift huts—which bizarrely resemble the house of Karagiozis, the famished and clever hero of Greek shadow theater, and which remind me of the poverty from which Greeks suffered until the 1950s—there are other, more solid dwellings of clay, brick, or cement. The most opulent-looking have roofs of corrugated iron, that is, they don't give the impression of wealth. Yet they have bars on the windows and are watched over by guards. All the outer walls are crowned with shards of bottle glass that keep the memory of French colonization alive: they are fragments from bottles of Bordeaux and Burgundy. Anyone who would even consider climbing over these walls to rob these houses must be very, very destitute. Bangi distrusts its residents enormously. It's a city in which destitution covets poverty.

It's true that part of the population possesses neither bed nor board. I've seen people taking naps almost anywhere, in particular on the edges of the traffic circle in the city center, which is surrounded by a large, empty, completely dry basin. Bands of children in rags asked me repeatedly for money, calling out the first word of Sango that I learned: *baba*. Because I wasn't used to hearing myself addressed in this way, it took me a while to realize they were speaking to me. I did what I could for them, within my means. The dictionary, which had warned me about the existence of street children, helped me to free myself from their grip. It whispered the word *nginza*, "money," to me, which allowed me to improvise the sentence: *Mbi yeke na nginza pepe*. "I have no money," or, literally, "I am with money not."

The smells of cooking at last made me hungry. It was four in the afternoon. On a table with trestles someone was selling small white loaves of bread and tins of sardines. I bought one of each and began searching for a place to sit. Suddenly I remembered the river. Although I had always considered it to be the main attraction of my journey, I had totally forgotten about it during my stroll. Someone indicated the direction I should take. The prospect of eating my sardines on the bank of the Ubangi gave me wings.

The city is built not far from the river. As I walked on, there were fewer and fewer houses, traffic dwindled, noises diminished. The trees grew to be gigantic. I could see the Ubangi around a bend in a road, behind a row of trees. It seemed as big as a lake, and as gray and still. Not a ripple disturbed its surface. Mesmerized by the river's immobility, I stayed atop the grassy hill that fell off steeply almost to the water's edge. I was equally entranced by the silence of this immense expanse. I squeezed the dictionary with my fingers, as if to call its attention to the vista. "Ah, but you know this place," I thought. "You were born here." I sat down, placing it next to me. Its yellow color took on an odd sheen amid the grasses. "You feel better here than in Paris, don't you?" I asked it. But it really wasn't a question.

Across the river sat a few hills with peaceful contours. They were so far away that I barely glanced at them. There was no sound of gunshots. "The Ubangi has only one bank." Its tranquility freed me from my preoccupations, my memories. My mind wandered aimlessly on the water, for the sheer pleasure of wandering. I thought of my mother, who had dreamed of knowing the world, and who would have been overjoyed that I was here, in this spot.

I was really not expecting to see anything, so I recoiled when I noticed a pirogue. It was filled with sacks that must have been very heavy, for it was almost under water. The man steering it seemed to be sitting on the river itself. He was holding short oars whose flat ends imitated the shape of a leaf. His wife, seated in front, also gave the impression of floating. She had a parasol like the ones printed on the cloth in Marcel Alingbindo's office. The pirogue, its cargo, and its occupants were much less visible than the parasol, which was bright red and seemed to be moving forward on its own, above the Ubangi.

I had begun to eat my sardines, using a crust of bread as a spoon, when suddenly some children shot out from behind the curtain of trees, raced down the hill, and ran to the landing stage about thirty meters away. Their clothes were the same as those of the street children, yet their faces were different: they had removed the dismal, vindictive mask they wore in the city. They were there to have a good time. Some of them took the trouble to undress, others threw themselves in the river with all their clothes on. Twenty times I watched them climb up on the landing stage, they were so happy to dive off. They would bump into one other, trip each other, laugh. I was lucky to see one of them perform the game whose description I had read in the dictionary, slapping the surface of the water hard. In so doing he produced a noise that was not quite that of a drum, but that resonated with a muffled sound. I noticed he made a bigger hollow of his hands right as they came in contact with the water so as to capture a little air in his palms. The Ubangi's role is to make the city dwellers forget their condition and give children back their true faces. I considered myself lucky to have chosen a language born on the bank of a river so kind.

The restaurant is called Couleur Café, like Serge Gainsbourg's song. It has white plastic chairs like the ones you find in Greek tavernas at the seaside. We dine outside, beneath a metal awning, while an orchestra composed of a saxophonist, a drummer, and an old guitarist plays softly in the background. The old man is the leader of the group; he also sings nostalgic songs in a velvety voice. It feels like we're on a cruise ship. He even dares to perform a few dance steps between verses. He's as skinny as a rail and is wearing clothes that are much too wide for him. They float on his body like a flag on a pole that has seen better days. Twice he has sung Henri Salvador's version of "The Lion Sleeps Tonight," and here he goes again:

> In the jungle, the mighty jungle
> The lion sleeps tonight.

Does he like this song so much? In any case, the French customers like it; perhaps they see it as a hyphen between the world they have left behind and the one in which they now live. One of the waitresses also likes it. She is wearing a very short skirt. I can see the restaurant's subdued lights reflected on her thighs. She goes to the microphone and sings with the old man:

> Hush my darling, don't fear my darling
> The lion sleeps tonight.

The French are thrilled. They take up in unison the onomatopoeia of the chorus:

> A-wimoweh, a-wimoweh, a-wimoweh, a-wimoweh.

This explosion of joy distresses Yves. His compatriots' elation depresses him. He consciously ignores them, looking instead toward the opening that has been made in the trellis around the terrace. Yet he knows these French people well, they all greeted him when they arrived an hour ago in their huge four-wheel drives. He didn't think it necessary to introduce them to me, with the exception of one man, Roger, the owner of the restaurant La Marmite, a handsome man with silver hair, wearing a gold medal of a lion around his neck. I suppose I'll only get to see these animals in the form of objects or images. The label of Mocaf, a brand of beer produced in Bangi, depicts an elephant's head.

Sammy is listening to the song with a faintly amused look on his face. He lived in France for a long time before returning home and being named inspector of schools and then minister of education. He is sixty-four years old. He never knew Psimis, the minister of Greek origin, but he remembers the Dimitris street corner very well.

"Everyone called it that when I was a kid. It became the Boganda street corner after independence. Dimitris's shop disappeared."

He raised his glass to the singer, who points to me and rolls his eyes. He sends the waitress to us, and she asks Sammy something.

"He wants to know if you're French," he says.

I could never resist the temptation to shine.

"*Kodoro ti mbi Geresi!*" I said to the waitress.

She goes to give the singer the news. He says a couple of words to his musicians and immediately they set to playing, all together and more energetically than before, one of Georges Moustaki's songs.

Obviously, I am touched. Do I think of this song as some sort of hyphen linking the stages of my life? The old man gestures to me, he wants me to accompany him! I answer that I cannot, that I don't want to. "Another day, maybe," I tell him, making half-circles with my index finger, but he still doesn't understand. Once again Sango jumps in to save me:

"*Kekereke!*" I cry. "*Kekereke!*"

There. He has understood.

"If you're going to sing tomorrow, I'll come listen to you!" Sammy says.

According to Yves, Sammy is very famous in his country, for having been a minister and as a writer. The author of many short stories and a novel, *The Witch's Belly*, published in France, he is nonetheless not a prisoner of his reputation. He is not a solemn man. He is able to do things that contrast greatly with his starchy appearance. He went right ahead and took off his shoes as soon as we sat down at our table, explaining simply that they hurt him. He definitely has a taste for serious discussions, but the slightest thing can loosen him up. He told me to use the informal *tu* with him at the start of the meal, as spontaneously as Samba had before him.

"Why doesn't he sing in Sango?"

There are several black people among the customers. They are all dressed in suits and ties despite the sultry weather, sultrier even than in the afternoon, it seems to me. What memories do these old French songs evoke for them? The foreigners are rather sloppily dressed. Only one old man is elegantly dressed, in an immaculate white shirt and linen trousers. I see him in profile. His forehead is dangerously close to his beer glass. Is he sleeping? His hands, resting on the chair's arms, tremble incessantly. Those hands will wake him.

"The French come here to dream," says Yves. "They spend their time imagining their return to France. Their favorite topic of conversation is the price of real estate in Paris. They imagine buying an apartment in the Montparnasse neighborhood, or sometimes a house in Deux-Sèvres.

"They're cheerful," Sammy states.

Yves takes a deep breath, as if the atmosphere were oppressing him.

"They are hopelessly like the French settlers described in bad novels. It's true. They're only interested in money and girls, they look down on the Africans, they often have a criminal record, and they drink enormous amounts."

The menu has remained open on the table. It is written entirely in French. The threadfin kebabs I ordered, following the dictionary's advice, proved to be delicious.

"I haven't seen a single word written in Sango since I got here," I commented.

"We never learned to write in our language," Sammy said. "There are no textbooks in Sango, our schoolteachers have not been trained to teach it. To introduce it into the schools would demand a considerable effort that our politicians are not willing to make. They know they need Sango to communicate with the people, and yet they don't always master it very well themselves. Their French is better. To allow Sango to be taught would mean to recognize the people's right to speak. Most of the students have difficulty with French, which they hear for the first time when they're about six years old. Only the most gifted among them manage to master it."

"You're in the same situation as the French when they had to choose between classical Latin and the vernacular."

"Is it necessary to choose? Languages are not inclined to fight one another. They are open to dialogue. The progress made in one benefits another. According to an experiment I carried out when I was with the Ministry of Education, students who study Sango at the same time they study French become better in French than those who are learning only French."

The old man dressed in white has stood up, putting his weight on his cane. He walks with difficulty. The waitress in the miniskirt takes him by the arm and supports him all the way to the restaurant door. There they separate. She has just offered a phantom up to the night.

"Who is that?" I asked Yves.

"Vincent Sibierski, a Frenchman of Polish origins. He must like it here because he has been coming every night for years, maybe even for decades. He never drinks anything but half a glass of beer. They say he was one of the construction supervisors for Bokassa's coronation ceremony and that with his own two hands he made the thrones on which the Emperor and his wife sat for the occasion. Since he rarely says a word, people think he has secrets."

"I'm going to hear so many stories that I will never be able to sleep again."

"I'll be leaving soon," he added. "I rarely stay out so late."

He has a small, sad smile. What does he regret exactly? Not having done what he usually does, or not breaking his habits more often? My father's fleeting smile was a real smile. It expressed deeper joy than what he allowed to appear. Either because he was modest or tactful, my father was content to give only a slight hint of his pleasure. I would be very unhappy if I were to forget his smile one day.

"We have no publishers in Bangi," says Sammy. "What would I do with a story written in Sango? Even the newspapers only publish texts in French."

Yves suggests that I read *The Witch's Belly*.

"Sammy drew his inspiration from an actual event that occurred in the 1920s in Banda country: all the inhabitants of a village died from sleeping sickness. In the novel, they attribute their tragedy to an old woman whom they accuse of witchcraft and they decide to punish her. But they are too dazed to execute her promptly. The old woman's lynching takes place in slow motion, it lasts an entire day."

Sammy listens with lowered eyes.

"And why the title?"

"People say that witches have a special organ in their bellies, blackish in color and of indeterminate shape. When someone who is believed to be a witch dies, sometimes her stomach is opened to verify if she was suspected rightly or wrongly."

"Wrongly, of course."

"Obviously."

The musicians had gone away for a moment and were coming back on stage. Sammy asks Yves if the photocopy machine in the French Cultural Center has been repaired. He wants to give me a photocopy of his book, of which he only has a single copy remaining.

"It's not in very good shape," he warns me. "It's even missing a page."

A car stops in front of the restaurant. Its headlights project the lozenges formed by the trellis onto the back wall and onto the orchestra, which is performing *Autumn Leaves*. It's playing more and more softly, as if it were moving farther and farther away, as if it were kilometers away. The old man is no longer singing, he's strumming his guitar, sitting on a chair. A fat fellow in a pearl gray suit rushes toward us.

"So, Gilbert, this is when you show up?" Yves reprimands him coldly.

Gilbert collapses into an armchair, calls the waitress in a breathless voice. "Esther, a beer!"

Then he turns to Yves. "I don't like it when you speak to me as if I were a child."

They are more or less the same age. Perhaps they have known each other forever?

"Forgive me, I'm exhausted. I want to go to bed. Let me introduce you to Mr. Nicolaides."

Gilbert explains to me that he is in charge of my trip to Sorcerers' Lake, that he has obtained the necessary authorizations, and that we'll make the trip together in a car loaned by the Ministry of Culture.

"I gave the minister a memo in which I told him that you had won a prize from the Académie française. Is this right?"

I thank him as warmly as my strength allows, for I too am exhausted.

"If I understand correctly, they're going to leave us here by ourselves!" he says to Esther. "You're not sleepy, are you?"

"Of course not, Monsieur Gilbert!"

While she is opening his beer for him, he caresses her thighs. His hand is plump, his fingers slender. I hope that Esther is going to rip one of his ears off with her teeth. But no, she doesn't react.

"Is she a *pupulenge*?" I ask Sammy discreetly.

My question overjoys him.

"Where did you get that word?"

"I found it a long time ago."

We walk a short distance in the dark. The telephone service where I will be able to obtain the cards I need for my cell phone is next to the restaurant. The streets, which the people have deserted, resemble vacant lots. Is the African night as dense as they say? What's certain is that the street lighting is very inadequate. The rare glow from the street lamps is so weak that it barely manages to reach to the ground. Sammy knows a retired journalist who gives Sango lessons. He'll put me in contact with him. I look up at the sky. It seems much more distant than everywhere else.

At six in the morning a cool breeze is blowing on the hill, giving me the illusion of being in the Cyclades, on the terrace of the house I had built there, facing the sea. I breathe in, closing my eyes. The air is slightly damp, like sea air, yet it is filled with another perfume, one that I don't know and that perhaps is coming from the forest. I say to myself that the wind spent the night on a bed of leaves. I attempt to decode it, to understand its message. I compare it to a mailman making his morning rounds.

The day after my arrival, I set the table that was in my room in the garden, two meters from the kitchen window. I also brought down my books, Marcel Alingbindo's lessons, and my notebook, because I was determined to work every day until eight o'clock. But in truth I work very little. I write a few lines, I absent-mindedly leaf through the dictionary. I spend most of my time just delighting in being here, with a mug of coffee at hand. Admittedly, I miss the sea somewhat. I am so used to contemplating the horizon that I am surprised to never see it here. The tall trees rising behind the fence and the singing of the birds nonetheless console me a bit. I hear thousands of birds, but I rarely see any. I suppose they are just fine where they are. The sound of their songs is so deafening that I wanted my friends to hear it. I called them all and said "Listen!" and then held my cell phone up to the forest.

"It's magnificent," Alice commented.

Jean told me that Sandra is pregnant and that they're getting married before Christmas.

"Can you believe it?" he said. "My son is going to be born in 2000!"

I offered to buy him an African mask as a wedding gift. I had forgotten he had got rid of his collections, that he had emptied his place out.

"I'll bring a bow and arrow for your son."

I had noticed that there were bows and arrows for sale at the market, as well as slingshots for bird-hunting. Georges told me that he had a surprise for me. He didn't want to tell me anything else about it. Yorgos asked me if I had already had an "adventure."

"No," I replied.

I hadn't yet slept with Esther.

The birds' concert begins at 7:00 AM on the dot, like a radio program. I listen to it attentively, as if it were a newscast. The birds give me the news of the day.

The ground in the garden is utterly bare, as it is everywhere else. Every now and then I make sure to take a closer look at it. I can believe that all the panthers have left, but I'm not so sure the snakes necessarily followed suit.

Samba is discretion itself. He busies himself about his hut without ever coming on my side of the yard. Our dialogue is limited most of the time to these two sentences:

"*Mbi bara mo.*"

"*Bara mingi*" (greetings many).

He gets up much earlier than I do, for by six he is already hanging out his laundry. It was by observing these clothes that I discovered he had a wife and child. He told me his wife works in the city and leaves the house at dawn, bringing the child with her. One day I discovered the boy high up in a palm tree, which allowed me to try out a new sentence:

"*Mo sara nye?*" (What are you doing?)

He was placing empty food tins beneath the branches in order to collect their sap, which is used to make palm wine.

Only after lazing about for a good half hour did I get down to work. That morning the dictionary was taken over by ants. I had left it open on the table and countless ants were wandering about on its pages. They were no bigger or blacker than typographic signs. In fact, at first I thought it was the signs themselves that were moving. No, it was indeed the ants to-ing and fro-ing, running between the lines, stopping on a period or a comma, encircling a w. I imagined that they thought the letters were a new people whom they intended to get to know, and that they considered the w to be a member of the nobility. I chased them away. Will they return? They must be quite intrigued by this motionless people. They probably think the dictionary is a necropolis.

At eight o'clock, as the sun erases the last traces of the sky's grayness, I go to the Phoenicia, carrying along my notebook and phone. I always take the same route; I get real pleasure from seeing the same shopkeepers along my path and greeting them. One sells postcards: they are mere sheets of white paper, illustrated with handmade drawings or butterfly wings that have been cut and pasted. Another is selling worn schoolbooks, among which I notice a French spelling book entitled *No Mistakes*. The third is a tailor who is also a shoe repairman. I'm hesitant to entrust him with my shoes, which have become unstitched, because I don't have another pair with me. He solves this problem by lending me his own sandals, which I wear for the entire morning. I meet a café owner who has the same kind of icebox that appears in Jacques Tati's *Jour de fête*, and a grocery store owner who displays his packets of cooking salt and flasks of palm oil on the ground. The orange color of the flasks is so similar to that of the ground that it is difficult to make them out. Central Africans often wear shirts, boubous, and *pagnes* of this same color. Esther was wearing an orange dress the night she came to the house. It's a color I'm beginning to appreciate.

I quickly acquire habits in order to forget that I'm here only for a short time. I strive to slip into the skin of a long-time city dweller who leads a very regular life. So I always sit at the same spot on the terrace of the Phoenicia and read the papers. They're sold by young men who could be students. I buy them all: *The Democrat, The Citizen, The Swallow, The Innovator.* They usually have the format of a sheet of typing paper. Some are photocopied. Their poor quality doesn't keep them from vehement polemics. With the exception of *The Innovator*, which is sympathetic to the government, they all call Patassé a terrorist, a dictator, a renegade, and a crook. They say he is a godfather in a mafia with international branches, who helps himself to the country's diamonds and gold. The freedom of expression that these newspapers enjoy proves that they are not widely circulated. According to Albert, they are hardly read outside of the central city. The vast majority of the population gets its information only from the state radio that broadcasts in Sango. *The Innovator* offers advice to people applying to emigrate, under the title "How to Emigrate Easily to the United States." I remember similar articles that used to be published in the Greek press. I read the papers with as much attention as if my fate depended on President Patassé's decisions.

From time to time I look out at the people passing in the street. I have been in Bangi for five days and I have the feeling I know them. I know where they live. I have seen them preparing their meals, seen them bathing their children. The products they sell reveal another slice of their existence: they are manioc growers, fishermen, hunters, iron workers. I hear their voices. It's natural for them to shout, they have things to sell. Bangi's population is not made up of silent shadows, elusive, mysterious, like that of Paris or Athens. It is transparent and surprisingly joyful when you consider its destitution. A taxi runs out of gas. Twenty people volunteer to push it. They do it laughing. Even the driver is laughing.

The more I observe them, the less I notice the color of their skin. When I'm in Paris or Athens, I'm hardly aware that the people around me are white. And now I'm learning that there are no blacks in Africa. There are only blacks on the other continents. Their skin is simply the mourning clothes they don when they go abroad.

I told Yorgos that the women were beautiful. Every morning I realize that they are even more beautiful than I had thought the previous day. Even the women wearing traditional clothing take great care of their appearance. Their shoes are sparkling, their hairdos sumptuous. Sometimes they adopt a hesitant, lazy way of walking. It's as if they are on a stage they don't want to leave. Many circle around the Phoenicia, where the customers are well-to-do blacks and Europeans. Are they waiting for an invitation? Their ballet constantly crisscrosses that of the beggars and the handicapped. This café, where I go so willingly, is at the same time a place that weighs on me. In general I stay only an hour.

I had my first Sango lesson on Tuesday at eleven in the morning. Albert, Sammy's friend, had made an appointment with me at the Hôtel du Centre, a very long, one-story modern building. He was waiting for me in front of the entrance, sitting on the steps. I thought he was asking for alms because he was wearing a suit as crumpled as Jackie Santini's raincoat.

"Mr. Nicolaides?"

He invited me to sit next to him, which put me in a wonderful mood.

"We're not going to work here, are we, Albert? Isn't there a bar inside?"

There was one, but he confessed that he preferred to avoid places where you had to spend money.

"You understand, I haven't received my pension in sixteen months."

I immediately paid him for the first lesson and told him he would be my guest.

"*Singila mingi, baba,*" he said to me, folding the bills carefully.

He explained to me that *baba* is a term of affection and that it can be used to address children as well. I'm starting to think that Africans lose weight as they get older. Albert is as slender as the guitarist at Couleur Café. His face is deeply lined, but this in no way spoils the sweetness of his expression.

We found ourselves on a kind of patio decorated with clusters of flowers and large green plants, with a kidney-bean-shaped pool at the center. Three young black girls in bathing suits were chattering at its edge. We sat in the shade, next to a picture window that overlooked one of the dining rooms. The air was almost as cool as it was in the morning in the garden. It seemed to me that I had never seen flowers as colorful as the ones here, nor women more ravishing than the three bathers, nor a face more moving than Albert's. For just a second my father's features replaced his. A turquoise blue and canary yellow lizard, infinitely more graceful than the small reptiles that visit my house in the Cyclades, appeared on the tiles, crossed the line of shade and stopped in the sun, three meters from our table. I thought back on the months I had spent cloistered in my Paris apartment. I considered that I, too, had crossed through a zone of shade and shadow.

"*Mbi yeke nzoni mingi,*" I told Albert.

He ordered a beer. I did the same, just to be able to clink glasses with him. I asked him if Sango was his mother tongue.

"My parents spoke Gbaya," he said. "I was born in the west of the country. My father, who was a shopkeeper, knew

Sango. The French and Italian priests who lived in the region taught us our Catechism in Sango. I came to Bangi when I was about fifteen. In high school, in addition to French, we studied English, Latin, and Greek. But the city itself spoke only Sango."

He hadn't become passionate about the language until 1960, when independence was proclaimed.

"This upheaval did not affect the situation of French, which has remained our sole official language. Yet it allowed for news bulletins to be broadcast in Sango on the radio, where I had been working since 1958. We realized that the language had considerable gaps. Even the word 'colony' was missing. So we undertook to reinvent it. This task occupied me for forty years, until I retired last year."

I told him about my meeting with Marcel Alingbindo.

"You know Marcel?" he shouted, jumping out of his chair. "We worked together for years, despite the geographical distance separating us. I commented on his proposals and he corrected mine. We used to call each other every day!"

"What did you find for 'colony'?"

"*Kodoro-va*, 'servant-country.'"

"You are poets."

"Not at all! We look for solutions that exist, that are already there in a way but that no one has yet recorded. The language predicted its own evolution. Marcel must have told you the same thing. Sometimes I would spend an entire night looking for a word. I would constantly focus on the hole I wanted to fill. I would examine it, probe it, interrogate it. I was almost always rewarded for my efforts. It is so pleasurable to witness the birth of a new word just before daybreak!"

The three young women had sat down two tables from ours. A large black man about fifty years old and dressed like a prince came to join them. He greeted Albert somewhat condescendingly, with a slight nod of his head.

"Four glasses of champagne!" he ordered loudly.

"He's an ex-prime minister," Albert whispered to me. "Do you know how long it's been since I've drunk champagne? Since Bokassa's coronation!"

He had a mischievous expression that made one forget his age. I thought his suit must be from about the same period.

"How do you want me to begin the lesson?"

"Maybe we could start with swearwords. I only know one, *pupulenge*."

"I'm not going to tell you all of them! There are some that are really obscene. *Buba* means 'idiot.' *Mo yeke buba*, 'you are an idiot.' We took the word *fou*—'crazy'—from the French, but we elaborated it, enriched it. We added three syllables to it! It became *fufulafu*! Don't you think it expresses madness better in this form?"

I jotted down notes in my notebook. I felt a genuine satisfaction in re-immersing myself in the study of Sango, which I had interrupted well before my trip to Greece. Albert was leaning forward to read what I was writing. Our foreheads were nearly touching.

"'Homosexual' is often used as a swearword. 'He's a *koli-koli*,' we say, meaning a man who goes with other men, or else a *koli-wali*, a 'man-woman,' an androgyn. A homosexual woman is called a *wali-wali*, a woman attracted by women, or a *wali-koli*, a 'woman-man.'"

He chose his words carefully, avoided repetitions, the way one does when writing. "He likes the French language as well," I thought. The ex-prime minister ordered a plate of smoked threadfin. I saw a huge gold ring shining on his hand. He must have had jelly jars filled with diamonds in his safe. I also ordered smoked threadfin and two more beers.

"What is the most obscene swearword that you know?"

I took the initiative of using the familiar *tu* with him in order to move our conversation away from propriety. Albert took a large swallow of beer and then said, "Your mother's clitoris! It's an insult that dates back to the time when excision was systematic. Women who still had their clitoris were considered to be prostitutes. But don't think I'm going to translate it into Sango for you!"

In fact, I had absolutely no need for this term of abuse. He taught me another, which also is applied to prostitutes: *gba-munzu*. It literally means "one who mates with the white man." Having heard the French say *bonjour* time and again, this word, slightly altered (*munzu*) took on the meaning of "white person" in Sango.

The terrace was becoming livelier. Well-dressed black men, accompanied by young and not-so-young women, some of whom were dressed in multicolored *pagnes* and white blouses, were sitting down to eat lunch or have a drink. I asked Albert if he knew of a photographer's studio on the rue Paul-Crampel.

"I don't recall a studio on that street.... It's not far from here. It runs behind the Maison de la Radio that was bombed by the French army during the May 1996 uprising when the rebels had taken control of the building."

"Marcel tells me that it is possible to make a sentence understood without saying it, solely by humming it."

"That seems difficult to me. There are hundreds of words that are accented in the same way. Most verbs belong to the deep register. But we can try if you want. Do you have an expression in mind?"

154

I had one, of course, but since I didn't want to make a mistake, I preferred to take out from my wallet the piece of paper on which Marcel had written, stressing the accents, *bàbá tí mbi à kúi*. I whistled ten times *do, so, so, mi, do, so, do*, without any result other than attracting the attention of a few customers. Albert had lowered his head, the better to concentrate.

"If I had some idea what it was about, perhaps I could guess what you are saying."

"It's about my father."

I began again, with the same eagerness as before. I wanted so badly to make myself understood that I was ready to spend the whole day on the experiment. But it wasn't necessary.

After a few moments, Albert exclaimed, "Your father is dead?"

A look of utter dismay crossed his face, as if the event had just taken place. I lowered my head in turn. The lizard had left. Two musicians arrived and sat down next to us, and this helped me to regain my composure. Albert's expression remained unchanged. I thought it my duty to comfort him: "He was very old, Albert."

One of the musicians had a guitar, the other a drum. They began to play even more softly than the band in Couleur Café. They sang a duet.

"In our country, there is a tendency to attribute death to occult causes, evil spells, or curses. A death is a crime that calls for an inquest, requires a guilty party. I know a woman who spent a fortune to avenge her daughter, who had died of AIDS. She didn't contest the reality of the illness, yet she was convinced her daughter would never have fallen ill if she had not been bewitched. The person designated as the guilty party is ordinarily a defenseless old woman who sometimes doesn't even try to defend herself. She, too, may believe that she is possessed by the *likundu*, an evil spirit. Now there's a word you need to learn."

"I know it," I murmured. "I read it in Marcel's dictionary."

The beer had put me in an odd state that I couldn't manage to define. I was simply obsessed by my inability to put my finger on it. "I must read Sammy's novel," I thought.

"Our society sees evil everywhere. It fears its own shadow. Did you notice that people often look behind them in the streets? The echo of the slightest nocturnal sound bounces off every object and ends up taking on fantastic proportions. We are afraid of cats."

"The Greeks are afraid of cats, too."

The musicians had the same repertoire of French songs as the ones I had heard on the first night. I thought that sooner or later they would sing *Autumn Leaves*, and I asked Albert to translate the last line of the French phrase, *tout doucement sans faire de bruit*, "very softly, without making a sound." He took my notebook from me and wrote, "*Yekeyeke, na wuruwuru pepe.*"

"*Yeke* means 'quietly.' It's pronounced like the verb 'to be,' both syllables are deep. By doubling it one gets the meaning 'very quietly.' *Wuruwuru* designates commotion, hubbub. You will note that *pepe*, the negating adverb, always comes at the end of the utterance. *Na wuruwuru pepe* can be translated as 'with noise not.'"

I thought it was pointless to mention that I already knew this rule. I turned toward the musicians and suggested that they slip these few words of Sango into Prévert's lyrics. I showed them the notebook.

They accepted enthusiastically, and they sang the bilingual couplet with great spirit:

156

Mais la vie sépare ceux qui s'aiment
Yekeyeke, na wuruwuru pepe!

I saw faces light up with joy. The waiter went to station himself next to the musicians, the better to hear the chorus. The end of the song was greeted with applause. The ex-prime minister's girlfriends were in heaven. He, too, applauded ostentatiously. I offered to buy the musicians a beer.

"I'll have another one as well," Albert said with that mischievous expression that made him appear younger.

Across from the Hôtel du Centre two wooden stalls have statuettes of elephants and women with pointy breasts on display, like the ones you find in Parisian marketplaces and on Trocadéro Square. There are also pictures made out of wooden rings arranged more or less symmetrically on a support. The only things worth noting about these little stores are their signs, which demonstrate a distinct sense of humor: one of them is called Au Bon Marché, the other Galeries Lafayette. I wasn't attracted by anything they had for sale or by the diamond wrapped in a piece of paper that a little boy showed me, so I wandered over to the shops that blocked off the end of the street.

They were fish stalls, a multitude of little fish stalls all wedged together, in front of which wood fires were burning. They were selling raw, fresh fish—which allowed me to discover the relationship between threadfin and perch—as well as grilled and fried fish. I assumed that the river must not be far, and then suddenly I saw it: it was behind the shops, twenty meters or so down. My joy was as great as if I had come across a long lost friend. The ancient Greek custom of personifying rivers seemed entirely reasonable to me. I wanted to drink a cup of coffee in its company to enjoy its presence a little longer.

The last of the fish stalls was run by a young man who didn't seem like a professional. I found him inside his shack sitting in front of a long table doing his homework. You could see the Ubangi from there because the back wall of the shack was only a half-wall. He was willing to make me some instant coffee, after which he immersed himself again in his books. The place was situated so close to the steep slope that led straight to the river, and so resembled Charlie Chaplin's house in *The Gold Rush* that I refrained from moving too much for fear that the shack would topple over the edge. The river was much livelier than it had been on Sunday afternoon. Several pirogues were meandering along it, their frail outlines fading into the water's luminosity. From time to time they would dance in the wake of a motorboat, continuing to sway long after it had passed, as if they were sorry the party was over.

"What are you reading?" I asked the young man in a hushed voice.

"My biology lesson. I'm studying the reproduction of algae. Algae are cryptogams."

This word affected me deeply, not only because of its scientific character, but especially because of its Greek roots.

"Cryptogam means 'that which joins in secret!' 'One who weds on the sly!' In modern Greek, the game hide-and-seek is called *cryfto!*"

Was I feeling the stirrings of nostalgia for my mother tongue? The appearance of a Greek word in such an unlikely place as a fish stall in Bangi was no doubt a sign.

"Algae reproduce in two phases. They lay eggs, like hens!"

We began to laugh at the same time. He laughed by making sharp little cries and banging his fist on the table. I imagined that our excitement would wind up plunging the shop into the river, which only increased my elation.

Once we had calmed down, we introduced ourselves. His name is Joseph. His father went into exile in France after having escaped an assassination attempt. He belongs to one of the river peoples, the Yakomas, who are systematically persecuted by Patassé, a man from the North. Patassé's main rival, General Kolingba, is Yakoma.

"My father lives in Montrouge," Joseph tells me.

His mother works for the customs bureau but only draws her pay once or twice a year.

"The fish stall supports us. We have good customers. Monsieur Bidou buys his fish from us."

I realized that his notions about Greece were as vague as mine about Africa had been a few months earlier. I invited him to the discussion that was to take place that evening at the Youth Center in the Boganda neighborhood. Yves had put the two events — the one that had been scheduled for writers and the other for students — together. But Joseph wasn't free. He had to stay at home to take care of his brothers and sisters.

"Do you have a lot of trouble with French?" I asked, switching to the familiar *tu*.

Among the books on the table I thought I recognized *The Art of Conjugating French Verbs* by its red cover.

"Yes, with the verbs. You don't use the simple past form, do you? You'd never say, for example, *je cousis*."

I almost had another laughing fit; however, the serious look on my host's face convinced me not to. He was truly expecting an answer. Perhaps I needed to laugh more than I needed to cry.

"No, we don't use it, except when we claim to be making 'literature.' But professors are hostile to the language's evolution. They are too attached to the simple past and the imperfect subjunctive to accept their decline. They desperately try to keep alive a word as moribund as 'refrigerator' under the pretext that *Fridgidaire*, the more common word in French, was invented by a manufacturer. They are arrogant, for they think they know better than the language itself what is good for it."

I finished my coffee, which was a little too sweet, and got up to leave. I had sufficiently disturbed Joseph in his work. And I have to admit that the smell of fish was making me a little dizzy.

"I'll come back and visit you one of these days."

"Good-bye, *baba*," Joseph said.

I returned to the Hôtel du Centre. Just when the porter was explaining to me how to get to the rue Paul-Crampel, the old Polish man whom I had noticed at Couleur Café passed in front of us, accompanied by the receptionist who helped him down the stairs. He was still dressed in white and was sporting a panama hat and sunglasses.

"Just follow Monsieur Vincent," the porter told me.

I let Monsieur Vincent take the lead and then followed close behind. He was gripping his cane more firmly than I had imagined him able. Forced to walk as slowly as he, I had a tendency to mimic his gait, rounding my back and leaning on an imaginary cane. I took a breather every three meters or so. "By the time we get to the rue Paul-Crampel, I'll be an old man." We passed in front of a ravaged building missing part of its walls and blackened by smoke. The shacks that followed weren't in quite as bad shape, but they had all lost their roofs. At the end of this alley, Monsieur Vincent turned right. There was a pole with a plaque on it here, a slight distance from the house on the corner. It was facing the direction of the perpendicular street. I was so sure that I would read the name Paul Crampel on it that I approached it with the thrill of a pilgrim arriving at his destination. And indeed that was the name I read. Yet I wasn't nearly as touched as I had been when I had located it on the map of Bangi while I was still in Paris. I also turned right, and found myself face to face with Monsieur Vincent.

"Are you following me?" he asked, his voice choked with anger.

He struck the ground with his cane repeatedly, each time raising a miniature cloud of dust. I gave him the explanations I owed him, without managing to calm him down.

"And just why are you so interested in the rue Paul-Crampel?"

"I'm looking for a photographer's studio that probably no longer exists, the Studio de Paris."

"You want to go to the Studio de Paris? Really?"

It was as if he were happy to observe my disappointment. "It's ridiculous to be mean at that age," I thought. He leaned against a tree and cleaned his glasses with a white handkerchief. His eyes were gray. His cane had fallen to the ground, and I picked it up, somewhat grudgingly.

"I shall show it to you."

We fell in step and from then on I walked at his side. The street was deserted. There were no shopkeepers in little wooden shacks. Even the huts were few and far between, separated by large vacant lots being used as garbage dumps. Two dead rats were lying in the middle of the road, flattened by a car.

"Voilà!" he said, satisfied.

With the tip of his cane he pointed to a windowless and doorless one-story house, in front of which was a courtyard with no wall around it, where the rusty skeleton of a car was lying. Four hooks were fastened above the entrance, vestiges of a vanished shop sign.

"The Studio de Paris has been in this state for almost forty years. Its owner went back to France in the early sixties. This is his car. To whom do the walls belong? It doesn't really matter, for, as you can see, they are reduced to dust. Dwellings in this country are conglomerates of dust. They always end up being swept away by the wind."

"Thank you," I said, to cut him short.

I didn't like the contemptuous pout that punctuated his sentences, nor his drawl, nor the theatrical way he rolled his r's. I was waiting for him to leave so I could explore the remains of the Studio de Paris in peace.

"All right, then. Since you are no longer in need of my services, I shall go," he said bitterly. "Still, I shall come to hear you speak Saturday. I was told that even the Empress Catherine is going to honor you with her presence. Try not to make too many foolish remarks."

Not only did he know who I was, but he knew my schedule even better than I did. Yves hadn't yet told me that my conference at the Cultural Center's library was scheduled for Saturday. I recalled that Bokassa's wife's name was indeed Catherine. I would finally learn if she had recovered her diamonds.

I went into the Studio de Paris. What was I expecting from this visit? The apartment was made up of a series of three linked rooms and two storage closets. Was it in the back room, the most spacious, that the photograph of my grandfather had been taken? The floor was littered with rubble and chunks of plaster. There remained almost nothing of the wall-covering save a few yellowish splotches on bricks of clay and straw. I began to rummage through the rubble, first pushing it around with my foot, then going through it with my hands, without finding the slightest trace of the pasteboard lion. There was an iron, a clothespin, a bakelite plug. My sole satisfaction was the discovery, in the entrance hall, of a black and white postcard similar to the ones Clotilde would send us for New Year's and which had contributed to my stamp collection. It was lying on the floor. It seemed so fragile to me that I didn't dare touch it. I got down on my knees to take a closer look. I saw a clergyman seated comfortably in a kind of wheelbarrow pulled by a black teenager. I blew on the picture to test its resistance. Immediately it disintegrated into a thousand pieces that flew away, wispy as butterfly wings.

It was already pitch dark when I left my house to go to the Youth Center. The trip to get there was not long. The Boganda neighborhood is located on the other side of the presidential residence, and the Youth Center is on the continuation of the street that runs in front of the Palace.

"It's a rather recent, octagonal building," Yves Bidou had explained to me. "You'll recognize it easily."

I meant to take advantage of this stroll to think about my lecture.

I wasn't alarmed by the humidity or by the wind that was producing an impressive trembling of the leaves and crackling of the tree branches. I judged it to be no stronger than the one that blows in the Cyclades in August.

I heard the first rumble of thunder as I was striding down the hill, but it was far away. On Place Valéry-Giscard-d'Estaing a second peal rang out, this time much nearer. I had a hard time lighting my pipe: the wind had suddenly picked up. The sheet metal roofs, which were doubtless not firmly fastened, were flapping everywhere. The city was swathed in a strange, pale green glow, similar to hospital lighting. It was not coming from the street lamps, which were fitted with white neon tubes. Perhaps it was coming from a place where night had not yet fallen.

As soon as I had started down the asphalt road leading to the presidential residence, I felt the stirrings of anxiety at the sound of a roar that the canopy of heaven amplified to infinity. I had the distinct feeling that this racket would awaken *Nzapa*, the god of rain, and yet for all that I didn't think I needed to run: I was quite happy to get to know the African rain. I had no idea of the magnitude it could take on. The author of Tarzan's adventures doesn't bother much with bad weather.

The palace guards took refuge in the sentry boxes. The first drops had just fallen. A single one was sufficient to snuff out my pipe. I put on a sprint but it was too late. I couldn't see anything. The rain had already obliterated the palace, the sentry boxes, the houses across the way, the street itself, and had extinguished most of the street lamps. It filled the space around me so completely that my movements were slowed and I had to close my eyes. Yet I could hear perfectly. I was less panic-stricken by the water than by the sound it made as it hit the ground. I thought I was listening to an army in flight. The rain did not make the wind die down, as it did in the Cyclades. It spun around, pushing me every which way.

Soon my feet were in mud, and I realized that I had gone off the asphalt roadway. The Youth Center couldn't be far now. This conviction gave me the strength to take a few more steps. I collided with a plastic sheet, beneath which a bit of light was filtering.

"Anybody here?"

No one answered. I lifted the plastic and passed my head inside a shack no different from so many others that line the roads. An old man was lying on a straw mat, his head resting on his bent arm, his eyes turned toward an acetylene lamp burning on the floor. He didn't seem concerned about the water that had flooded part of the floor, and only had eyes for his lamp. I asked him where the Youth Center was located. He didn't budge. I repeated my question.

He raised his left arm to indicate a direction, without turning his eyes away from his lamp. "He thinks it will go out if he stops looking at it." It seemed indispensable to me to hear the sound of his voice to assure myself that I was in the presence of a real human being, but I couldn't think of a question to ask him. Lacking inspiration, I wound up by saying, "What weather we're having!"

He answered me just as simply: "I'll say!"

But not once did he look at me.

I thought I had nothing more to fear from the rain. In any case, I was already soaked to the bone. When I caught sight of the octagonal building, I even stopped walking. I thought that *Nzapa* was, in spite of appearances, a merciful god and that he had let this amazing storm loose to help me forget the gentle Athens rain that had made me so sad back in March.

The room in which the meeting was to be held was a classroom filled with old school desks. It looked more like a cloakroom. The people who were waiting for me had half undressed and were drying themselves with rags or paper and laying their shirts out on the furniture. The class was very joyful. Only Yves Bidou seemed anxious.

"You absolutely must change out of those clothes, you'll catch your death!" he said before running out of the room.

With each step I took I made a pretty little puddle on the floor.

"They look like ellipsis dots," quipped Sammy, who was sitting at one of the desks in the first row.

Sammy had removed only his shoes. He hadn't yet managed to make me a photocopy of his novel; the machine at the French Cultural Center was still out of order. He was thinking about using the one at the Department of Education. "I'll never read his book," I thought.

Behind him a man about his age with curly hair and big glasses was feverishly writing in a datebook. A journalist from the local television station came to greet me; he was naked from the waist up, wearing a towel on his head. He asked for authorization to film the conference on Saturday. Yves joined us, carrying an astonishing pair of blue pants and a yellow shirt borrowed from a theater troupe working in an adjacent hall. The colors reminded me of the lizard in the Hôtel du Centre. I put on this get-up, not without pleasure, and without the slightest embarrassment. I didn't feel like I was among strangers.

The atmosphere was certainly not favorable to an in-depth discussion. The rain, drumming tirelessly on the roof, was making almost as much noise inside as out. From time to time there was a sort of explosion. I imagined that the Congolese army had taken advantage of the storm to cross the Ubangi surreptitiously and had laid siege to us. Sammy reassured me: the explosions were caused simply by mangoes falling on the roof.

While Yves was citing my books, I was looking at the ellipsis dots that were slowly shrinking on the floor. He didn't leave out a single book, not even *The Shipwrecked*, which hadn't been reprinted since it was first published. I wasn't at all convinced that our audience had any interest in Doctor Remlinger and little Martine. I myself felt no delight in coming across these characters again. I simply regretted not having begun anything new since *The Tin Soldier*, and having given up writing for so long. Yves's praise seemed excessive to me. When he stated that my writing seemed spontaneous, that it seemed more like oral speech than like writing, I almost interrupted him: "I take great pains with the least little sentence, Monsieur Bidou." He had discovered certain resemblances among my characters that I had never noticed. I didn't remember that one of Monk Gaspard's sisters suffered from the same lapses in memory as Doctor Remlinger. The remark that intrigued me the most, however, had to do with my old stamp collection. He assured me that I had mentioned it in three of my novels. For a moment I was charmed by the idea that the point of departure for everything I had undertaken in my lifetime could be found in this collection. I even wondered which country came after French Equatorial Africa in my album. He concluded with a clever remark, declaring that my bedside books were probably dictionaries because I wrote in two languages, to which Sango had recently been added.

Several people were taking notes. The man sitting behind Sammy, however, had stopped writing. He was the first to ask a question. "In what language do you think?"

"When I'm in Greece, I think in Greek. When I write in French I think in French. I can't say which language I would favor if I stayed on a deserted island for a long time."

"I think it would probably be Greek," said Yves.

"I think in Sango and I write in French," the man said.

Sammy turned around to respond to him. "Not so, Adrien. When you write in French you inevitably think in French. The words that you write reflect your thoughts."

"I assure you that I elaborate my projects in Sango," the other man insisted.

"Why don't you write in Sango?" I asked him.

He raised his arms to the sky in a sign of impotence. "Who would read me in Sango? French gives me access to a real audience, it transmits my ideas infinitely."

We heard an ominous crack, as if the mango tree itself had crashed down on the roof. "Tomorrow there will be no more houses or trees in Bangi. The water and wind will have carried everything away. The survivors will go out to hunt for their city. They'll find it in the end, but so far from its present location that they'll have to give it another name."

A man in his forties, seated among the students who had gathered at the back of the room, stood up.

"I published a small novel in Sango," he stated. "There indeed exists an audience for Sango, as long as the books are inexpensive."

"You found a publisher?" asked Sammy, surprised.

"The first books published in French were crude brochures," Yves reminded everyone.

I told them that until the 1960s Greek popular literature was mostly distributed as fascicules, sold in newspaper stands. "They were adventure tales that sometimes took place in the jungle, but also love stories between Greek bandits and Ottoman princesses.... May I ask you what the subject of your novel is?"

"It's called *Queen of the River*. It's about a very beautiful young woman whose lower limbs are paralyzed. She is saving her money in order to buy a pirogue. She tells herself that when she'll go out on the Ubangi in her pirogue, people will not notice her handicap, they'll only see her beauty."

"I'd like to read that," Sammy told him. "You should send it to me. Do you indicate the tones in your writing?"

"I only use two accents, like Alingbindo."

168

"You don't indicate the modulated tone?" asked Sammy.

I questioned him about this, as I was unaware of its existence. He was kind enough to explain to me that the last syllable of a sentence sometimes requires a double inflection of the voice, ascending or descending.

"This modulation has its importance. For example, it allows you to indicate irony, to make someone doubt the seriousness of what you just said."

"I'll wind up regretting not having learned Sango," Yves commented, once again with his sad smile.

Sammy and the author of *Queen of the River* agreed that the written form of Sango shouldn't be made overly complicated.

"You write in a language that has not yet reached maturity," I remarked to the author.

"It leaves me freer than French. It's not burdened with references, it encourages improvisation. And at the same time it allows me to speak about the Central African Republic better than I could in French."

"What about you?" Sammy asked me. "Do you see a difference between the stories you tell in French and those you write in Greek?"

"I suppose I wouldn't use two languages if I said the same thing in both. The sea appears more frequently in my Greek texts. My mother tongue returns me to the fold, a little like Sango led me here. Still, I don't think my writing changes from one language to another. If I thought it did, I would give up one of them. I translate myself quite easily."

"I find that you talk about languages very dispassionately," said a student sarcastically. "Have you forgotten that French was the instrument of our enslavement? That this language constantly whispered to us that our culture was almost worthless, that we were less than nothing? That it managed to convince us of this, because we continue to repeat its point of view? I left school too recently to have forgotten the punishment I suffered when I began to speak Sango in the schoolyard. No one put a bone around my neck like they used to, but I was obliged to write, 'I shall no longer speak in Sango' a thousand times. I cannot love a language that imposes silence on me."

Despite the patter of the rain, one could hear him panting.

"When did you begin to write in French?" he asked me.

"In the early 1970s. At the time, Greece was governed by a military junta and I could not express myself freely in my mother tongue. I had no bad memories in French. I was even more at ease in the French-language novel because French uses so many Greek words. But writing in a language that your mother doesn't understand, that doesn't share your memories, is not bearable for long."

Yves ended the discussion somewhat abruptly. Was he in a hurry to go home again? He announced my lecture at the library of the Cultural Center with affectation. Adrien closed his date book and vanished without saying goodbye to anyone. When we left, Sammy, the student, and the author of *Queen of the Jungle* were in a heated discussion.

"Gilbert is waiting for you at the Riviera," Yves said when we had climbed into his car. "He wants to go over some of the details regarding your excursion to Sorcerers' Lake."

The rain continued relentlessly. The car sent up great splashes of water as we drove. We hadn't made a single comment about the discussion. He just asked me why I hardly mentioned my father in my books.

"I never had lengthy discussions with him. He didn't express his feelings."

The entrance to the Riviera was guarded by two huge muscle men.

"Why don't you come with us?"

"I prefer to go home in the evening. The night is not my friend. So many things can happen at night."

Gilbert was slumped over in one of the little booths that surround the dance floor, accompanied by Esther and another girl. There were already six empty beer bottles on their table.

The other girl's name was Delphine. She was resting her head on Gilbert's big belly. Esther was wearing a skirt even shorter than the one she had worn at Couleur Café. It was, in other words, as if she were naked.

6

I spent the better part of Friday waiting. First I waited for the car from the Ministry of Culture that was to take me to Sorcerers' Lake. It was 5:30 in the morning. Among the clothes that Samba was hanging out were three of my shirts. I felt like I had found a family.

At six o'clock I saw a small dump truck drive up. Three people were in the cab: the driver Faustin, a counselor from the Ministry of Culture named Nicolas Bingaba, and Gilbert. A fourth character, a soldier armed with a machine gun, was standing up in the back of the truck. It was explained to me that the roads outside Bangi were very unsafe.

"The countryside is filled with bandits," said Gilbert, who was wide awake.

They gave me the spot next to the driver. I unfolded the map of the Central African Republic on my lap. I was eager to reach the crossroads where the road splits in two, one side leading to Crocodile Lake, the other to Sorcerers' Lake. I was preparing to tell Faustin, "This is where you turn right."

But I had to be patient. At six o'clock the entire city is up and about, and it's bursting with traffic and business. Already meat and shrimp are being grilled. The children are on their way to school. The peddlers are already on the job. They sell cigarettes by the piece, like they used to in Greece. Have I come here to resurrect my past? I think about it so often here that there are moments when I have the disconcerting feeling that Africa remembers me.

For the first time I noticed a lot of people waiting at the roadside. They were not carrying anything, they had nothing to sell. They didn't seem tempted to go in one direction or another. The place they wanted to go was probably inaccessible on foot.

We were moving quite slowly, not only because of all the traffic but also because Gilbert would stop the car every time he spotted a pretty woman. He would run to her, talk to her for a few moments, take down her phone number, and come back to the truck bright and cheerful, showing us his slip of paper:

"Hurray! I got it!"

"If you keep this up, we'll never make it to Sorcerers' Lake," I warned him.

The night I spent with Esther had created a kind of complicity between Gilbert and me.

"Can you explain why it is that you want to see this lake so badly?"

I couldn't, of course. We were stopped for quite a while in front of the morgue. The road was blocked by people yelling, crying, ululating with heartrending grief. A woman was hopping from one leg to the other. Sorrow was causing her to dance. Nicolas went to find out what had happened: the police had killed a young criminal.

"The chief of the anti-crime squad is a murderer," he explained to me. "He executes young hoodlums with a bullet to the head or shoots them in the back. Often he leads them through the city before he kills them to make them regret life's pleasures all the more. This happens in the early morning. Then he tosses the corpse in front of the morgue. Usually the families don't press charges so as not to drag their name through the mud, and because they fear reprisals. It's rare that they mourn so loudly. The young man who is going to be buried was sixteen."

Death also rises early in Bangi. It took me some time to recover from this piece of information. I wasn't very happy when we arrived at the road signs pointing to the two lakes. "I'll never be able to take the same route to the center of the city again," I thought. Nicolas told me that the person in question had his headquarters in the Central Police Precinct, next to which I passed every day.

"Bokassa was content simply to cut off the ears of thieves in public," Gilbert said. "His cops made the hoodlums lie on the ground and mutilated them with machetes. They put the ears in bags."

"Where did they do that?"

"At the central traffic circle, fifty meters from the Phoenicia."

The picture of Bangi I had painted in my mind was in the process of wheeling around like an opera set, revealing its dark side. Conrad's exclamation "The horror! The horror!" came back to me. I started to breathe easier only when we arrived at Damara, seventy-six kilometers from the capital.

We parked on an esplanade of beaten earth that was as big as a soccer field and where only two buildings were standing, very far from each other. One was the city hall and the other, the sub-prefecture. And there we waited some more. I asked about the purpose of a long metal crate mounted on a hand-cart: it was used for carrying caskets. I thought it would have been very handy for my friend Stanislas.

A little old man appeared at the far end of the esplanade. He was coming toward us so slowly that I got tired of looking at him and even forgot about him until he was right in front of me. He wanted to see the mayor. His suit was in worse shape than Albert's. He waited with us, but since the mayor didn't come, he decided to leave. With calm steps he took up the path that led back to the horizon.

We needed the mayor to sign our travel warrant. When at last he arrived we followed him down a corridor where the signs on the doors were written in French: "secretariat," "deputy mayor," "mayor." The only things on his desk were a little Central African Republic flag and a paperback edition of a *Larousse* French dictionary.

We also had to go through the sub-prefecture. The sub-prefect was a tall, slender woman with refined manners, wrapped in a magnificent yellow *pagne*. She received us rather coldly, deeming that we should have come to see her first. "Dumas would have written an entire novel about this woman, entitled *La dame de Damara* (The Lady from Damara)."

The chief of the last village before the lake, who was a re-tired postal worker, kept us for over an hour on the veranda of his house. We drank palm wine. I can't say I like this viscous drink with its strong aroma. I had the ridiculous notion that it tasted like old furniture. We spoke about Sorcerers' Lake, which in reality is called Sorceress's Lake.

"According to legend, the lake is the work of a sorceress who drowned all the inhabitants of her village to avenge the death of her son, who was killed during his initiation. At the clos-

175

ing celebration of the ceremony, she drew a circle around the dancers with a broom that had been dipped in a potion she had made. And this is how the lake was formed."

Many people were listening to him, for several peasants had come onto the veranda. Gilbert was the only one who wasn't. He was incredibly bored, no women were anywhere to be seen. If he wasn't yawning it was only because the air was infested with gnats. I was so afraid they would enter my nostrils that I was trying to breathe sparingly.

After a short pause, the village chief continued. "They say the musicians are still playing their instruments at the bottom of the lake. On some days soft music wafts from the waters. They also say you can see the goats' tails that traditionally adorn the initiates headdresses floating on the surface. But personally I have never seen or heard a thing."

It was noon. I began to lose all hope of ever seeing the lake. The closer I got, the more it receded. Besides, was it worth it? Neither Nicolas nor Faustin had ever seen it. I was just thinking that the day had been wasted when the chief gave the signal to leave. A moment later the entire population had climbed aboard the two available trucks, the chief's and ours.

"We've organized a little celebration in your honor," he announced.

I thought about the sorry folkloric events Greek hotelkeepers offered for tourists.

"Do you get many visitors?"

"Not too many. Seven years ago an Anglican pastor and his wife came to see us."

The grasses were becoming taller and taller. They hid the path, drooped across the hood of the cab, stroked its windows. They were all we could see, as if we were at the bottom of a lake. Then little by little they thinned out and were replaced by trees.

The vines that tied them together looked like telephone cables. "The trees use them to talk about the weather."

When I opened the truck door, I was struck by the deafening rumble of tom-toms accompanied by singing and the sound of whistles. The space was overflowing with music. I immediately felt the same exaltation I had felt as a child when on Sunday mornings I would head out to see Tarzan at my neighborhood movie theater. Once again I was ten years old. I felt capable of running as swiftly as an arrow flies. Africa finally appeared to me the way I had always imagined it: like a fantastic playground.

We walked to a clearing. The dust kicked up by the dancing women flew to the tops of the trees and played with the sun's rays. There were thirty or forty of these women, most of them very young, naked from the waist up, their lower bodies covered in leaves. They looked like overturned trees, leaves fluttering in the wind. The extremely rapid motion of their legs contrasted with the very slow movement of their torsos, which they lowered in small, mechanical jerks before rising up again. At the same time, they stretched their elbows in back of them. Some of them were blowing whistles like the ones policemen have. But most of the music was produced by four young men feverishly banging on their tom-toms.

One of the women wore a cross around her neck, another had attached a key ring to a braid of her hair. Gilbert examined them one by one, then went to sit at the foot of a tree. Their breasts, just beginning to form, could inspire no dreaming.

"Young girls used to do this dance after excision," Nicolas explained.

We went to sit next to Gilbert, who was following the meanderings of an ant. It didn't seem like it knew where it wanted to go. Nicolas offered some money to the village chief, who thanked him profusely. The amount, though, was extremely modest, the equivalent of about a hundred French Francs. Gilbert and I took the initiative to contribute as well in order to encourage the dancers, who had stopped dancing and were looking at us and whispering.

"They're nothing but children," Gilbert said, rather discouraged. "So are we going to see this lake of yours?"

We saw it. It is surrounded in part by a beautiful forest, so dense that it seems black even in daylight, but the lake itself is less pleasing to behold. It's brown. The chief couldn't explain why it had this strange color. "Maybe it has something to do with the witch's brew," he joked.

He tried to convince us that the water was clean, but we saw several dead fish that we had at first mistaken for goats' tails.

"There are crocodiles in there," he swore.

We didn't see a one. We were examining the water's surface when the music started up again. For a moment we thought it was rising from the lake bottom. I realized that it had already lost the power to make me relive a morning from my childhood.

"Are you disappointed?" Gilbert asked me.

"I think I'm starting to let go of Tarzan."

We ate on the veranda. Faustin preferred to eat his meal in his truck's cab. I had seen the work of a witch, now all I needed was to visit the den of a sorcerer. I had a tendency to confuse sorcerers and witch doctors. I remembered that the dictionary described the latter as both medicine men and poisoners. It seemed to me that this double role required an explanation, and I asked our host about it.

"It's true they wore two hats, even three, for they were usually excellent dancers as well. It was their job to find the sorcerers who were harming the villages. They would bring all the villagers together on the town square and denounce the guilty person. Since the poison they made him drink was supposed to spare the innocent, his death became proof of his guilt. Sometimes they would simply make the women do a ritual dance that was supposed to chase away the *likundu*. They danced naked, young and old, away from the eyes of the men. It is said that flames would come out of their mouths and their genitals."

I thought of the orange flames shooting from the mouth of the dragon Stanislas had painted.

"The Church and the authorities have fought against this part of their activity, which has died down considerably today. They still administer poison every now and then, but only to chickens and goats. The death of the animal obliges the suspect to make reparations for the injustice he has done. Still, people continue to call on witch doctors when they are faced with signs of witchcraft. To this day they are feared."

"Yet they are not sorcerers."

"How could they recognize sorcerers with so much certainty if they weren't sorcerers themselves? And as doctors they can be very useful. We have one in the village who has cured many people. He's from the forest. The best healers come from the forest. The old trees know many secrets."

"I'll go take a look." Will Nicolas and Gilbert agree to come with me? I noticed that the conversation seemed to interest them.

We ate grilled antelope, manioc, and python with vegetables. I hardly touched the python, even though it tasted like the octopus we eat in Greece. Despite the fact that the reptile had been cut into slices, I was loath to pierce it with my fork, as if I thought it were still able to react.

The young girls had gone back to the village. I could see them in the distance. They had formed a circle and were still dancing.

"You speak about the witch doctors very irreverently," I remarked.

"That's because my grandfather is a witch doctor. Their spells cannot touch me. They scratch the surface, but they don't harm me. I am protected by my grandfather's spirit."

"Perhaps my grandfather is protecting me, too," I thought, though without conviction.

"I doubt there is any country where the practice of magic doesn't exist," Gilbert declared. "In France there are religious sects that claim to cure every illness, even cancer. I'm sure that people believe in the evil eye in Greece."

My memory conjured up the anxious face of a woman who had accosted me on a ship's bridge to sell me the merits of the Orthodox Church. She admitted that she was seeking in religion a remedy for the spells that had been cast on her by her father's mistress. She attributed her bad health and the strange dreams she was having to this woman's influence.

"The only people I see in my dreams are people who are completely unknown to me," she confided.

"In the Berry region of France, in any case, they are absolutely convinced it exists."

Nicolas told us about a certain *nganga* who conducted very successful witch hunts. "Recently he dug up a canary and a heart oozing blood near the bus terminal. He claimed they had been buried by a sorcerer who wanted to harm the young people of the neighborhood. The *nganga* burned the canary and the heart in front of the crowd, which cheered him on. The people admire him, but it seems that the authorities do as well."

"Do you think I could see your medicine man?"

My request made the chief nervous.

"I'd have to let him know ahead of time. I should really send one of my sons. He lives on the outskirts of the village, but the hut where he works is near here. I'll show it to you. Don't count on me, though, to attend the session. He's not the same ethnicity as I am. He could take advantage of my being there to play a trick on me."

He wasn't so sure about his grandfather's protection after all. Nicolas and Gilbert got up without a fuss. The chief vanished for an instant, then led us to an isolated straw hut at the edge of a wood.

"He's extremely greedy. Don't give him more than fifty francs, no matter what."

"What's his name?"

"Teddy."

Once again we had to wait, this time in the shade of the straw hut that was five meters long and two meters high. The door was ajar, but we avoided pushing it open to peer inside.

Teddy came from the woods, where we hadn't expected him, so that suddenly he loomed before us. He looked like an Argentinean tango dancer disguised as a soccer player. He was dressed like the latter with the slicked-back hair, hatchet face, and jet-black eyes of the former. He was wearing a red jersey with an effigy of President Patassé on it and a pair of black shorts. He had the bowlegs of a soccer player and was wearing dancing pumps. He addressed Nicolas.

"*Mbi yeke tene na sango,*" he said, "*ngbangati so mbi yinga faranzi pepe.*"

For the first time ever, I had the great satisfaction of understanding an entire sentence: "I'm going to speak in Sango because I don't know French." Convinced that I would find this sentence useful, I memorized it immediately.

Nicolas offered to act as interpreter, and we entered the sorcerer's den, which was surprisingly bright. The light filtered through the bamboo walls and through the roof that had partly caved in. The furniture was comprised of three plank armchairs, an open wardrobe filled with bark and dried plants, and a very low wooden stool on which the master of the house seated himself. He lit a candle that was stuck in the flooring and contemplated the small dish that had been set down in front of his feet. It contained a few drops of water, a small crystal ball, a tuber with a branch stuck in it, and a translucent yellow globe. He was obviously concentrating very hard. He turned his gaze to me.

"*Nginza*," he said simply.

I gave him a 5000 CFA franc note, which caused him to make a disagreeable pout.

I doubled the sum, thinking that I would have paid at least a hundred francs for a visit to the doctor in Paris. I made him understand that I was ready to forego the consultation if he didn't accept this amount.

He slid the money beneath the plate and handed me the yellow globe, advising me to hold it firmly for a few moments. Then he made a sign for me to stand up and take off my shirt. He pushed his fingers into my stomach, my abdomen, and explored my lower back. He was disgusted when he sat down again.

He explained to Nicolas that I was suffering from a chronic illness that affected my kidneys, heart, and brain, making me immensely fatigued and reducing my sex drive. He emphasized the fact that only he could cure me and that I should come to see him often.

"Does he take me for a *buba*?"

"He needs to know your thoughts on the matter."

"Tell him that I'm not suffering from anything."

From the nasty glimmer in Teddy's eyes I could tell that he understood French. He stared at me, but I didn't lower my eyes. Then he changed his tune. He mentioned the *likundu* and declared that my neighbors were plotting against me.

"Tell him I live on a desert island and I don't have any neighbors."

His gaze grew nastier still. This was no doubt the gaze he leveled at the little old ladies whom he accused of witchcraft. I had a strong urge to fling some of the insults Albert had taught me at him. Surely he was wearing the same jersey Patassé supporters wore so he could get in good with the cops.

"Should we get out of here?" I said to Nicolas.

My abruptness calmed the magus. He offered me gifts of various bits of bark, advising me to steep them in hot water and to drink a glass of this concoction every morning. Gilbert did the best thing he could during this session: he fell asleep.

We got back to Bangi very late that night. The street lighting was even dimmer than usual. Many of the neon lights had gone out, probably because of the storm. The darkness seemed extremely dense to me. Was it because I was thinking of the killer who was the leader of the anti-crime squad? Was it because I could see Teddy's face again in my mind's eye? I was still filled with the wonder of the sound of the tom-toms, yet I couldn't get these sorry characters out of my thoughts. "This is a country where both young men and old women are in all kinds of danger."

Some streets were lit only by the fires that were still burning in front of the huts. Families were gathered around these fires and contemplated them, motionless. The groupings were so beautiful that I felt like I was looking at paintings in an exhibit.

But the painting that thrilled me the most was one of a young man who had set up a table beneath a streetlamp in order to take advantage of the electric light. In the deserted street, well after midnight, he was reading from a weighty tome.

I fell asleep thinking about this young man. The next morning, I gave the bits of bark to Samba to burn in the fire over which he was heating his palm nuts.

On Saturday morning, I scolded myself for having neglected that handful of Greeks who, according to the information I had gotten in Athens, still live in Bangi. It seemed to me that my grandfather, whose photograph was on my end table, was not smiling as much as usual.

"I'll try and find out if there are any members of your family still here," I promised him.

I also left his letter on the same table, as if I intended to read it of an evening or a morning. Truthfully, though, I wasn't very curious to learn its contents, which were not meant for me.

I began my inquiry by introducing myself in a large Portuguese grocery store. Its owner assured me that no Greeks owned any grocery stores in the city. But he recalled having dealt with a certain Tsiros, who managed a transport company, a few years earlier.

His directions allowed me to find Tsiros's company where — alas! — I was greeted by another Portuguese man who informed me that the company's founder had died. Since I had just learned about Tsiros's existence fifteen minutes earlier, his death seemed very premature to me. The new director didn't leave me in an awkward position for long: he knew of a Greek mechanic who repaired cars.

"His name is Scarvelis. His shop is at the edge of the city, on the road to the airport."

Once I got to the shop, which was at the back of a court-yard, I immediately recognized Scarvelis. He was small, stocky, and bald. Was it his handlebar moustache that allowed me to identify him? Or was it the mark left on the jaw by the language we speak?

The fact is I addressed him directly: "Are you the Greek?"

He looked me up and down and then, with the familiarity that the Greek language allows, asked me, "What cat dragged you in?"

His debonair attitude lacked sincerity. He was suspicious. Did he think I was needy, a beggar? I have to confess I wasn't dressed to my advantage. I was wearing a dusty tee shirt and an old pair of pants. When he realized that all I was asking for was a little of his time, he became downright cordial. He decided to close up shop immediately, putting everyone out — the employee from the American Embassy who was trying to sell him a used Mercedes, car owners who'd come to show him defective parts, a taxi driver whom he told to throw out his vehicle, plain and simple. He also dismissed his secretary, after having exchanged a few words of Sango with her. He spoke with the ease of an African. "I'll never learn this language that well."

"You speak perfect Sango," I complimented him.

"It's not a hard language. You could learn it in two weeks if you wanted to."

I felt slightly stupid, but I was delighted to hear these few Greek words. He led me to his house, which was right next to his shop. His resonant voice seemed to fade into the distance at sporadic intervals. It conjured up other voices, other faces. I noticed that the Greek words did not exasperate me, did not stir up my feelings as they had during my stay in Athens. I wasn't paying much attention to what Scarvelis was saying. I was having another conversation with my mother tongue.

After half an hour I had forgotten I was in Africa. Although his living room was filled to bursting with African statues, the language had put up its own scenery, brought in its own images. We were no longer in Bangi, but in Athens, or Mytilene, for Scarvelis was from Mytilene. It didn't take him long to pull out a bottle of the famous ouzo that's produced on his island, and he served it in large glasses filled with ice cubes.

"It's the water that makes our ouzo so good," he explained. "In my village, we use only rain water!"

We didn't speak much about home. He had left Greece at twenty, in the early sixties, and hadn't had many chances to return. He had arrived in the Central African Republic via Chad, where he had worked for one of his uncles. I thought that his move to Bangi must have caused him many more problems than I had had to adjust to Paris. He would never have adapted if he had not forgotten Greece.

"On my island they call me 'the African.'"

Apparently he didn't care one way or the other about that. Did he intend to go back one day?

"My wife is already there, with our eldest child. She left in 1996, during the riots. She got scared. If I could find someone to buy my shop, I would leave too, but I can't. My second son, who is here, unfortunately isn't interested in cars."

What he missed the most wasn't Greece itself, but the Greek community in Bangi, which was still flourishing in 1960. He was as proud of it as my grandmother must have been of the Greek community in Alexandria. He praised its members who, to hear him talk, each had a particular genius for something. One had made a name for himself in the grocery business (this was probably Dimitris), another in cultivating coffee beans, a third had excelled in the transportation business (I guessed he was alluding to Tsiros), a fourth had triumphed in the diamond business. The most brilliant of all had been that André Panayotopoulos about whom I had heard in Athens. He had not only built the first hotel in Bangi, but half the city as well. My grandmother would say similar things about how Alexandria owed everything to the Greeks.

"I am the last Greek in Bangi!" he exclaimed with a sudden zeal that was due partly, perhaps, to the ouzo.

I thought he was about to beat his chest like Tarzan. He confirmed that the community had died a natural death, unable to provide its own successors. He was nostalgic for Bangi. I thought the time had come for me to mention Clotilde Bérémian, née Nicolaides. When he learned that she had been my great aunt, he nearly hugged me.

"Why didn't you say so?"

I realized that from then on I could ask him for anything, even money. I limited myself to requesting only a few olives. He went to the kitchen and returned with a great quantity of food that he placed on the low table between us.

"I met Clotilde as soon as I got to Bangi. She would call me 'my little Scarvelis.' 'How are you, my little Scarvelis?' she'd ask whenever she would see me at her husband's factory. She was a real pioneer's wife, enterprising, brave, strong. Even when she was over seventy she could still climb up on the roof of her house to patch a hole. Once she almost strangled a little creep who had broken into her yard. The kid got away with his life thanks to a snake that had slid between Clotilde's feet. She crushed its head with a blow of her heel."

"She had almost become a man," I said, remembering my father's comments after she had visited us in Athens.

"She was tough, but not with me. Sometimes she'd give me Turkish delights. 'Here you are, my little Scarvelis, this is for you.' André was hard on his workers as well, whether they were black or white. He liked to joke, though. When anyone would trouble him with anything, he would always say, 'My name is André I-don't-have-a-cent.' Of course he was very rich. He practically had a monopoly on the production of nails in all of central Africa."

"He made nails?" I asked, surprised.

"Yes, nails, didn't you know?"

All that good food on the table didn't appeal to me. I only ate a few olives. He told me that Clotilde's and André's ashes had been transferred to Marseilles, to the Bérémian family vault, and that their daughter lived in France and their son in the United States. I asked him whom he saw outside of work now that the Greeks were gone and his wife was gone.

"I have a few Portuguese friends. I play *pétanque* with them on Sundays."

"You don't have any African friends?"

"Lord no! I see enough of them at work!"

"And yet you know their language very well. It could have brought you closer to them."

"I learned Sango because I had to for my business, not to chat with them!"

I ate another olive thinking it would be my last. What was there that remained for us to say to each other? I still needed to ask about the archives of the old Greek Consulate in Bangi.

"I've got them. You want me to show them to you? If the minister of foreign affairs wants them back, all he has to do is come get them. I have no intention of going broke sending all these boxes to Athens."

The archives were in four boxes labeled "canned milk," piled up in the basement. We contemplated them for a few moments in silence, with the respect owed to gravestones. "I certainly won't cry here," I thought.

"I can pull out a few files for you if you want."

"No, don't bother."

"In any case, the history of our community is in here," he added, slapping the top of the box.

His hand was immediately covered in dust.

Mario, his youngest son, a blond twenty-seven year old, was waiting for us in the living room. He told his father that he was going swimming in the Ubangi with some friends and that he would be back late. He didn't speak Greek very well.

"You see," Scarvelis said to me. "He's only happy in the company of blacks!"

"That's normal! I grew up with them! I'm African too!"

He laughed as he said that. His laughter was indeed that of a black man. Some day Scarvelis will speak to his son in Sango.

The people of Bangi had razed the old Cultural Center in response to the French Army's repression of the rebels in 1996. So it was in a brand new, spacious locale still smelling of paint, encaustic, and resin, that I was invited to speak before a large audience composed mostly of Central Africans. Yet the best seats had been set aside for the French. I recognized several people in the room. Even Esther had come; she was standing near the door as if she were thinking of leaving before the end. The television crew had set up in the aisle that divided the rows of seats in two. All the seats were taken, with the exception of a single one in the front row between the Central African minister of education and the French ambassador. It looked as if the two men were not on speaking terms. This wasn't the case, however, because they were in fact talking to each other across the empty seat. "They left this seat for my father, but he won't be coming."

Gilbert, who was in charge of hosting the event, said barely a word about my books. I had a strong impression that he had not read any of them. Nor did I think they could be found on the shelves of the small bookcases that stood a good distance from one another along the side walls. The *Grand Robert*, however, was there; I could see its nine volumes with their green bindings from afar. They reminded me of members of the French Academy in their robes, assigned with the task of monitoring my words. A little to disconcert them, and a little to disconcert the French people in the room, I began with the words that Teddy the sorcerer had pronounced, modifying them slightly:

"*Mbi yeke tene na faranzi, ngbangati so mbi yinga sango pepe* (I'm going to speak in French because I don't know Sango)."

Someone let out a cry of joy. I thought it was the student who had spoken at the Youth Center, but no: the troublemaker was none other than Vincent Sibierski. He was wearing a large red flower in his buttonhole.

I continued in French, although my sole subject was Sango.

"I heard the name of this language for the first time in Beauvais, at the home of an old man who owns many cats. His wife taught me that the word *kua* changes its meaning according to whether it is pronounced in a low tone or a high tone, that it means 'work' in the first sense and 'death' in the second."

The ambassador questioned the minister with his eyes to make sure this was so. Adrien had sat down in the first row, next to the ambassador's wife, a very skinny redhead with a pock-marked face. He had opened his date book on his lap and was still writing. "He only writes in public," I thought.

"Sango is probably more musical than either Greek or French. If I didn't know that it had been invented by pirogue boatmen, I would easily have thought it had been invented by dancers. The tones make learning the language difficult and are, at the same time, one of its main attractions. Sometimes I have thought I could detect a kind of complicity between the meaning of certain words and their music. The sequence of high, low, high, low tones meshes marvelously with the onomatopoeia *kekereke*, 'tomorrow.' That's a word that rings true, just like *nyau*, 'cat,' which begins on a high note and ends on a middle one. I confess I was shocked by the petulant music of the word *mbakoro*, 'old man,' which uses all three registers because its first syllable is middle, its second high, and its third low."

I realized I could talk forever on the subject. "I'm taking my oral exam in Sango." Not only did I want to pass this exam, but I experienced true pleasure in recovering these words, in traveling again along the path I had followed since I had discovered Marcel Alingbindo's dictionary and W. J. Reed's textbook. Yves Bidou was sitting to my left, Gilbert to my right. I had the distinct impression that the latter was less attentive than the former.

I spoke about all the aspects of the language that had enchanted me, from the prefix *a-*, which indicates the plural, to numerical adjectives that come after the noun, to the negating adverb that bursts forth at the end of a sentence.

"Sango forbids you to interrupt your interlocutor until he has reached the end of his thought."

I spoke about the modulated tone that cancels out, in its own way, the content of a sentence, about the verbs that have no need of the countless variations they undergo in French and in Greek, of the absence of the verb "to have."

"'To have trouble' is said 'to be with trouble,' which seems just as good to me."

Gilbert had abandoned me to sit with Esther. The ambassador's wife was yawning. The minister, who had also come with his wife, said a word or two to her from time to time. As for the ambassador, he was impassive. He was certainly used to being bored. Was I addressing the empty chair?

Still, I persevered. I spoke about the words that Sango had borrowed from the French and had transformed to suit it, words like *fufulafu*, or the ones Marcel Alingbindo and Albert Mawa had invented, like *bakari* and *kodoro-va*, as well as the translation for Snow White that the author of the dictionary had suggested. I sang the praises of the grace of young girls whose cheeks are the color of mangoes in rainy season, and of expressions such as 'You are pleasing to my eyes' or 'How many times will you sleep before returning?' I lamented the fact that the only Greek word adopted by Sango, *politiki*, had taken on such a detestable meaning. At last I recalled the words that had moved me the most, words such as *de*, "the cold," *mbasambara*, the number seven, and *pupulenge*.

The room had been somewhat lifeless until I pronounced this word. The Central Africans were exhibiting an unusual reserve. It seemed as though they were intimidated by the newness of the place. The event was unfolding in a way that was just as boring as if it were taking place in a Cultural Center in Deux-Sèvres.

Pupulenge was like setting off fireworks. It triggered such an explosion of joy, such an uproar, that the ambassador and his wife started to panic. "They are afraid of black people. They know that Africa doesn't like them."

"What does *pupulenge* mean?" the ambassador asked with a look of sheer terror on his face.

"Slut!" the minister replied.

I imagined my father seated between the two men. I thought that this scene would have delighted him.

"So you came, then," I said to him.

"I had to, didn't I?"

The laughter continued. Exasperated, the ambassador's wife got up and asked me this surprising question in a loud voice: "Is Sango a real language?"

Her question cast a cold spell over the Central Africans. One of them, the author of *Queen of the River*, took it upon himself to respond. He did so deferentially, rising to his feet as well: "Perhaps it is not a real language, Madame, but we have been using it for so long that we no longer ask ourselves that question."

Gilbert rushed to the side of the ambassador's wife with a portable microphone in his hand, but she gestured that she didn't need it. Several people then asked for it, the ambassador, Sammy, Albert, the student, the television journalist.

"What is Adrien writing?" I asked Yves Bidou discreetly.

"I don't know. He's never published anything."

Gilbert passed the mike to the ambassador, and he addressed his question to me: "Why did you decide to learn Sango?"

"Foreign words have surprising stories to tell. It's so pleasant to be with them. I was probably a little weary of always seeking answers from the same Greek and French words. I needed to hear something different from what I already knew. The Sango dictionary was just as fascinating to read as Tarzan's adventures had been when I was a teenager."

Gilbert gave Sammy the mike. "Is there such a thing as an uninteresting language? A language that has nothing to say?" It seemed to me that he was asking the ambassador's wife these questions, although he wasn't looking at her. "I don't deny that Sango has its shortcomings. It has difficulty adapting to the modern world, like our country itself. We have, however, linguists who are making every effort to overcome these insufficiencies. In my opinion, they should take more inspiration from our regional languages, Gbaya, Ngbaka, Banda, and Zandé."

The student intervened without waiting for the mike: "Linguists aren't the ones who make the language evolve, the street does. Young hoodlums have contributed more to its enrichment than academics. The words they create are so successful with the masses and with students that they continually have to come up with new secret languages. They went from 'double Sango' to 'triple Sango' to 'double triple Sango.'"

"I do not believe that street children are in a position to bring to the language the scientific and technical words that it lacks," the minister observed.

Did he sense that the question regarding the teaching of Sango was going to be broached soon? The fact is, he brought it up himself. "At its current state of evolution, it would be difficult to use Sango to teach certain subjects."

I thought about the tumultuous discussions that had taken place in Greece at the time when Katharevousa was still in use.

"Do you remember?" I asked my father.

He did. I thought that a polemic just as lively was about to begin when the author of *Queen of the River* told the minister in a virulent tone that the gaps in Sango were due precisely to the fact that it wasn't taught. "If you don't give it the possibility of rubbing up against scientific progress and new technologies, it will remain incapable of assimilating them. By refusing to let it have access to education, you're condemning it to falling behind, and that's exactly what you're criticizing it for."

I had never felt as close to Sango as I did then: I thought I could hear the beating of its heart. And so I entered the discussion without any qualms whatsoever. "In Greece, the supporters of the erudite language that had been imposed in the schools were of the opinion that the popular jargon was incapable of expressing the upheavals of the time. Ever since it has become Greece's official language, this jargon has clearly proven its ability to deal with every subject. I have the sense that, in the struggle between popular languages and scholarly languages, it is the former that always win. If this is the case, you could spare yourself a debate that poisoned Greek intellectual life for a century and a half."

Albert finally managed to take the floor. "In regards to that last comment, I'd like to add. . ."

His voice was slurred. He was nodding his head as if he were seeking the right distance from the mike to speak. He had clearly been drinking.

"I'd like to say to my friend Nicolaides, whom I admire greatly, for after all. . . ."

His eyes were darting left and right, trying to find a place to focus so that he could think.

"But he's wrong about this. . . Sango is not guaranteed to win. Dozens of languages have died in Africa. They die on a daily basis. We are a cemetery filled with languages."

Gilbert took the mike from him to give it back to the minister, but this didn't stop Albert from going on:

"They wake up in the middle of the night, exhausted. They've lost their voice. Every night they discover that they no longer have a voice!"

He would have probably collapsed if Esther hadn't intervened. She took him by the shoulders and helped him to sit gently on his chair.

"Sleep, *baba*!" she said to him.

Albert smiled gratefully and then shut his eyes.

Meanwhile, the minister affirmed that he was in no way hostile to the official consecration of Sango. "I only wonder if it's necessary to teach a language that everyone knows."

Now it was Sammy's turn to react vehemently. "No, my dear friend, we do not know it. One cannot know a language that one has not studied. I even think one has to study it continually."

I confessed to them that I had almost forgotten Greek in the years that followed my settling in Paris. "I didn't write it any more, didn't read it any more, and spoke it only rarely. It was becoming a foreign language. The only things I could spout in Greek were platitudes and commonplaces."

And then I turned once again to my father. "You're not too bored, are you?"

The room was filling with a kind of effervescence. The television crew quickly moved toward the entrance, a lot of people stood up. Vincent Sibierski crossed the room with the agility of a young man.

"Well," Yves said to me. "Here comes Dust from the Cold!"

She was wearing a long dress, as white as snow.

"Is that the empress?"

It was Catherine, the empress. She was moving slowly toward the front of the room, her head held high, a charming smile on her lips. Sibierski followed her step by step, with one arm extended behind her as if to protect her from being assaulted by assiduous admirers. The minister and the ambassador greeted her effusively.

"Am I late?" she asked absent-mindedly.

She must have been close to fifty, yet she was very beautiful. Her bare shoulders were exquisitely formed. "She's going to sit on my father's lap. Now he won't be bored at all."

"Is she the one who offered diamonds to Giscard?" I asked Yves in a tiny voice.

"Where did you read that?"

"In *The Three Musketeers*!"

Sibierski would not leave Catherine until he had forced the red flower that had been in his buttonhole into her hands.

"Though rumor has always had it that she had an affair with Giscard."

"Just like Anne of Austria and the Duke of Buckingham!"

"Exactly!"

The debate had trouble taking off again, but at last it did. Sammy suggested that the minister institute a national Sango day when the people would be invited to tell stories, recite poems, and sing in the street. The student believed that people found speaking French on that day should have to wear a bone around their neck.

"Ridiculous," the ambassador's wife murmured.

I made a request to the minister: to change the spelling of the road signs to conform to the rules of written Sango and to delete, for example, the *u* in Bangui.

"Forty years after your Independence, you'd think you would free your cities of their colonial veneer!" I lectured him.

He took no offense. On the contrary, he applauded both proposals. I suppose he was happy to get out of a prolonged debate about education.

"You haven't said anything about your work," remarked the ambassador, who must have had enough of the discussion about Sango. "What are you working on now?"

I rested my eyes on the empress, who was still smiling. She had not made the slightest movement since she had sat down, so I had the feeling I was looking at her portrait. I thought she must have had the same frozen expression during her husband's coronation as she sat in the throne that had no doubt been built with love by Vincent Sibierski.

"Not much," I acknowledged.

The television crew had moved in front of the first row in order to film the empress. The journalist asked me to say a few words of Sango, to which I gladly agreed since I remembered perfectly the three sentences I had prepared.

I saw him as I was reciting like a parrot: "*Mbi ye Beafrika. Mbi yeke nzoni na kodoro ti ala. Beafrika a nzere na le ti mbi.*"

My surprise was so great that I was almost at a loss. He was standing between the two bookshelves, his back to the wall. At first I thought it was merely someone who resembled him. His features were not familiar enough for me to be sure I wasn't mistaken, and he was tan, which changed his appearance considerably. It wasn't, however, by his face that I recognized him, but by his raincoat: Jackie Santini. He was studying me with a delighted look on his face.

I couldn't speak to him right away. Gilbert had just concluded the event. The minister congratulated me on my French.

"I'm very attached to the classical language," he confided. "I refuse to use the feminine of the word 'minister' in French. 'Madame Minister' seems so much more elegant to me! Don't you agree?"

Adrien and the ambassador agreed ardently with him.

"I share your sentiment," said the ambassador. "I prefer by far 'Madame Ambassador' to 'Ambassadress.'"

"And what about the English words that French adopts for no good reason?" Adrien added. "Did you know that the word 'songwriter,' in English, is now commonly used in *Le monde*?"

A scene just as mediocre was playing out a little farther away: Catherine was returning Vincent Sibierski's red flower to him.

"I cannot accept this, Vincent," she was saying to him.

"Oh, Catherine, Catherine," lamented the Pole.

"I am not simply going to let things run their course. I must give them a direction." I looked at Santini again. His intrusion seemed to be a mistake to me. "Why has he come?" I went toward him with a certain amount of animosity.

"What are you doing here?" I asked him rather sharply.

"I came because I had to come! Georges told me that you had decided to mention me in your next work! I imagine that the action will take place in Bangi? Well, I came to serve you. I am not one of those characters in novels who balk at my job, who are never there when you need them. Georges strongly encouraged me to undertake this expedition. Because I have to say, it's a real expedition to get here from Addis Ababa! I've been traveling for two days! I spent seven hours waiting in the Khartoum airport! Aren't you happy to see me?"

I didn't know he was so talkative. As quickly as it had appeared, my irritation gave way to a limitless benevolence, not only toward Jackie Santini, but toward everyone who was still in the room. I was worried about Vincent Sibierski, who seemed desperate; about Albert Mawa, who was certainly incapable of going home alone; about the ambassador's wife, who must have been humiliated by some of the comments.

"Of course I am! Still, you have to admit that it will be difficult to justify your presence in a book about Africa. Your being here risks seeming out of place, ringing false."

"But that's the whole point! The greatest authors use comic relief to brighten up their story! I'll be the funny note in your tale! My ambition isn't to play a big part. I don't claim to have the stuff of a hero. In any case, I'm returning to Paris tomorrow morning. I left my bags at the airport."

"Can you wait a few minutes? We'll go dine with the cultural attaché, the librarian, and a woman friend of mine."

I pointed out Esther, who was talking to Yves and Gilbert. "She's magnificent!"

She was wearing a tight-fitting red dress that made her body look like a flame.

The ambassador was speaking very highly of Giscard's presidency, perhaps in order to please Catherine.

"I know Greece very well," she said to me.

Vincent Sibierski was leaving by himself. He was walking with even more difficulty than when I had seen him for the first time at Couleur Café. Never before had he seemed so old to me.

The minister was explaining to Sammy that Patassé often calls him in the middle of the night.

"He starts working in the evening and doesn't go to bed until dawn."

"So that's why this country is doing so badly: Patassé makes his decisions at night." Sammy invited me to spend Tuesday morning at his house.

The author of *Queen of the River* and the student were helping Albert to stand up. He was dozing. Still, he managed to snap out of it long enough to say to me, "You are the most *undiligent* student I've ever had!"

Esther scolded me sharply for not having paid sufficient attention to her. Our adventure had cost me a small fortune.

"I've no more money, Esther."

"You're not my sweetie any more?"

"I'm not your sweetie any more. *Awe.*"

She didn't get angry. She had already spotted Jackie Santini.

"I'm surprised you didn't ask the empress for her phone number," I chided Gilbert.

"I already have it!"

We had reserved a table at the Hôtel du Centre. I told them that Jackie Santini would be coming with us.

"I was thinking during your lecture that by imposing French on the students we are not doing the language any favors," Yves said to me. "We are paying it a very poor tribute."

I preferred to go by foot to the hotel with Santini. He had in fact booked a room there.

"Why are you leaving so soon?"

"The next plane for Paris after that one leaves in a week."

"That's the plane I'll be on," I thought.

"Did you stay long in Addis Ababa?"

"Yes. I had a hard time persuading the mother to let her daughter leave. I only managed it in the end by doubling the amount that Georges had offered. As of now, the girl is in Paris."

"Is she pretty?"

"Not really. But she has a sweet smile."

I recalled that Georges had spoken to me about the girl's smile.

"It seems that her brother is just as greedy as her mother."

"The last I heard, he's changed his ways. He wants to open a used-book store, with Georges's help, naturally. Let's talk about your book instead. Is it moving along?"

"Not really."

"But you've got other characters besides me?" he asked anxiously.

"I'll definitely talk about my father.... And maybe about Georges, and my friend Jean Fergusson."

"What an excellent name! Still, it's already been used by Jules Verne. The head of the mission that flies over Africa in *Five Weeks in a Balloon* is the intrepid traveler Samuel Ferguson."

"My friend has traveled a lot as well."

"With Fergusson and Santini on your team, you are definitely sure to win! It's odd how traveling makes me want to play soccer."

"You should write that sentence in your notebook."

"I'll give it to you! If it can be of use to you, take it! I ask nothing of you in exchange. I know how to be generous, Mr. Nicolaides. I hope you won't forget to mention that!"

When we arrived in front of the steps to the Hôtel du Centre, I warned him that Esther would probably make advances to him, and that her offers of service had a price. I advised him to take the usual precautions. He was touched by my solicitude.

"It's only natural for me to look after my characters' well-being!" I declared.

"Mbangi is the name of a former tribe from the region. Sango is also the name of a tribe. My name, *Mbolieada*, means 'Who will not die?' in Zande. That's the question my parents were asking themselves when I was born because an extremely bloody war had broken out. Formerly we all had but one name that alluded to an event or a situation. Albert's name, Mawa, was chosen because of a calamity that had befallen his family. *Mawa* means 'suffering' in Sango. It's only recently that we have started giving children their father's last name and a Christian first name."

The house is large but there are so many inhabitants that it seems small. Sammy has seventeen children and about forty grandchildren, some of whom are old enough to get married. Not all these people live under his roof, but no one lives far away. Their courtyard is surrounded by small huts that house part of the family. The main room where our conversation is taking place is as bare as a convent parlor and as lively as a school. Doors are constantly opening, and there are always three or four people on the inside stairway.

"I've had four wives."

I met the youngest, who is half Sammy's age. I gave her a bottle of perfume.

"*Singila mingi, mingi, mingi.*"

We drink beer.

"My eldest daughter is older than my last wife. I have grandchildren who could be the parents of my youngest son, who is only eight. Sometimes I stop a child as he is going by and say 'Who are you?' I was born in a family of twenty-two children. You can't help feeling a bit like an orphan when there are so many of you who share the same father. Our state marriage allows us to choose between monogamy and polygamy. I know that churches don't approve of our customs, but they don't really hold them against us. The Catholic Church, which I attend, is more tolerant than the Protestant. Near Zemio, in the eastern region of the country, there is a prophetess who is as famous as the Pythia of Delphi, and who answers the questions of the faithful about the future. The priests allow her to deliver prophesies during the liturgy. It is said that she can walk in the rain without being touched by water."

I told him about the strong antipathy that Teddy inspired in me.

"I don't really like healers much either. I prefer to call on a priest when I feel like I'm in danger. A few years ago a family of owls decided to roost under the roof of my house. I had the parish priest come. He recited prayers in the four corners of the property and the owls cleared out. We consider them to be birds of misfortune."

"Their reputation is no better in Greece."

"Beliefs that aren't shared always seem childish. Are the pilgrims to Lourdes any less naïve than those who run to the *nganga*? I'm much less of a skeptic than Albert is. If I had had twins, I would have been sad. Here we often attribute supernatural powers to twins. We have a tendency to take them for sorcerers, who are said to have two faces, one for day and one for night. Still, I am crushed by our society's propensity to make accusations, to denounce imaginary crimes, by its taste for malicious gossip and its willingness to accuse others. Even though Adrien lived in France for ten years, he is convinced that every denunciation contains its grain of truth."

"Most of all I will remember a young man I saw studying one night beneath a streetlamp."

"Everyone should have access to electricity and to what it takes to live a reasonable life. We are three million in an immense country that has both diamonds and water. The Central African Republic is certainly much richer than Greece, yet the Central Africans run after you to ask you for money. We are a rich country inhabited by poor people. It seems to me that the main cause of our misery is the corruption of politicians. Our colonizers didn't bother to think about the country's future. They took what there was to take. We aren't sensible. We have more children than we can feed so as to appear less poor than we really are."

The children running around don't bother me. Victorine, his wife, brings us tomatoes that have been quartered, with salt and pepper, served just like in Greece.

"*Singila mingi, mingi, mingi,*" I say to her.

"Have you missed Greece?"

"I came across a compatriot and encountered my mother's sewing machine and a stairway similar to the one in my parents' house."

I consider asking his advice regarding my grandfather's letter: would he read it if he were in my shoes? I feel that it's up to me to resolve this dilemma, that I shouldn't shy away from it.

"Most foreign writers speak about Africa as if it were a nature preserve. They are primarily interested in its flora and fauna. Jean Guéhenno, who came here on an academic inspection mission around 1950, wrote in his diary that the French don't know the names of their black servants, yet they give names to their cats and dogs."

"Many tourists look on Greece as if it were an open-air museum. They're surprised to find that it's inhabited."

"I often have the feeling that we are still under colonial rule. We are helpless before the whims of the government, the police, the army. We are a land where human and civil rights are not respected. In the past, no one would complain whenever a French soldier shut off the television in a café because it bothered him. And today a police officer can do the same thing without provoking any reaction. We are a people without a voice."

"And yet you have a powerfully loud language, capable of making itself heard."

"Yes, that's true. We have music, but we don't yet have the lyrics to go with it. Sango is perhaps our last bastion. A people deprived of its language is a defenseless people. I've talked to Bidou about publishing short texts in bilingual versions. He could find the necessary funds to do it. Is it possible to change the language one writes in at my age?"

"The words will give you back the youth you had when you learned them."

"When I'm with my wife, I forget that I'm older than she is. I also forget that I'm older than my grandchildren when I play with them. Since I'm every age I've ever been at once, I'm annoyed always to see the same old man in the mirror."

Before I leave, I go into the bathroom. The door doesn't close properly, the flush doesn't work, the fanlight's glass is broken. This opening looks out on the back courtyard, where other huts are standing. In the narrow alleyway that separates them from the house, several women are washing, brushing their hair or braiding each other's, playing with their children, chasing a dog or a chicken. At the end of the alleyway, a girl about fifteen years old is ignoring the noise around her and writing equations on a blackboard set on an easel. She has filled it with miniscule signs, completely incomprehensible to me. She's wearing a light-weight flowered slip.

Of course Sammy could not photocopy his novel. He'll send it to me in Paris, as soon as he has found a machine that works. We say goodbye, touching our foreheads together, twice on one side, once on the other.

Tomorrow night I'll take the plane. It's scheduled to arrive in Paris on Monday at 6:00 AM. According to Gilbert, the temperature almost everywhere in France has fallen below freezing.

"You're going to freeze your. . . ," he said.

I've gotten a severe sunburn. Yves gave me some cream that I'll continue to apply once I'm in Paris, in the cold. It will remind me of Africa. Everything, it seems, will remind me of Africa, including the pain-reliever I take for headaches, called Doliprane. I haven't forgotten that "elephant" is *doli* in Sango, and I don't imagine I ever will.

In fact, I feel as if I'm experiencing a beginning rather than an end, as if my journey were going to continue for a long time. I don't foresee giving up studying the Sango dictionary. It has imperceptibly lost its exotic character. From now on, its words will be part of my own story. I haven't been able to write the words *Baba ti mbi a kui* without feeling something for a very long time. I cannot pronounce, or even whisper, this sentence with serenity. I no longer read the dictionary as if it were some adventure novel, but as if it were an autobiographical tale. I'm sure I'll eventually wind up putting it on the shelf next to the *Grand Robert* and the Greek dictionary. And yet I'm convinced that I'll continue to open it from time to time, to get the news, the way you call a former lover whom you once adored.

I gave W. J. Reed's textbook and one of my own books to Joseph, the boy who sells fish by the river.

"It's not enough to know a language, you still have to learn it!" I told him emphatically, voicing one of Sammy's opinions as if it were my own.

I got undressed in his shop and left my clothes with him, then went down in my underwear to the river where I took a swim. I swam slowly, trying not to make waves, as if I were in a dream and were afraid of breaking it off if I moved too suddenly.

Without realizing it, I had swum away from the riverbank. I greeted a boatman in a pirogue: "*Mbi bara mo.*"

"*Bara mingi,*" he said to me.

I wished him a good trip: "*Gue nzoni.*"

I was as proud of this exchange, however brief, as if the boatman had given me a gold star in Sango. "I can now claim to know the language because I have spoken with a pirogue boatman." But my illusion didn't last long, for a moment later the man was heaping insults on a motorboat driver who had almost overturned his small craft. I didn't understand a word of what he said. There must be loads of insults that Albert didn't teach me.

Before getting out of the river, I gave a friendly slap to the water, without managing to produce the drum-like sound.

According to Joseph, the flowers growing along the river belong to a siren who chooses during the day which swimmer she will go to at night. To my great disappointment, I had no visitors that evening.

I took leave of Albert at the Hôtel du Centre. We drank two glasses of champagne. He told me precisely the opposite of what he had said at the library, that Sango will continue to gain ground at the expense of French, and that sooner or later its victory was guaranteed.

"A few years from now, the only place French will be spoken will be within our Ministry of National Education!"

He confirmed that *sara mbeti*, "to form a letter," was also used to mean "to write."

"How would you say 'I write in Sango'"?

208

"'*Mbi sara mbeti na sango.*' If you want to emphasize that the action is really happening in the present, it is better to say '*Mbi yeke sara mbeti na sango.*' *Mbi sara mbeti* evokes the past, 'I have written,' 'I wrote.' Similarly, *Lo yeke gue* is translated as 'he is leaving,' and *Lo gue* as 'he has left.'"

"How would you say 'my mother and father have left'?"

"*Mama na baba ti mbi a gue.*"

When they left the Congo, the French apparently abandoned countless mixed-race children whom they had had with local women.

"In Sango, the term 'mixed-race' is rendered by the expression 'stay-in-the-Congo,' *ngba-kongo.*"

I wanted to know if he still remembered any of the Greek he had learned in school, if he could recall one word. He thought for quite some time. His expression became almost pained.

"Don't tire yourself, Albert. It's not that important."

Suddenly he shouted, "Thalassa!"

And this is how my last Sango lesson with Albert Mawa came to end on a Greek word.

One morning I awoke with tears in my eyes. I hadn't had a nightmare, not even a dream. I wasn't even sad as I opened my eyes. And yet my face was drenched in tears.

Another day I was woken by a bird that must have been in the tree whose branches touch my window. I listened carefully to its song, which played on three notes, a middle, a low, a middle, a high. "He's telling me something in Sango," I thought. Several times throughout the morning I tried to reach Albert by phone to ask him about this mysterious message. I couldn't manage to reach him, so I called Marcel Alingbindo in Poitiers.

"Several interpretations are possible, of course," he said after having noted the four tones.

I heard him burst into laughter.

"Do you know what the first one that came to my mind is? 'Where are my slippers?' The accentuation of this sentence matches the bird's song perfectly!"

"Little Louis must have stolen his slippers again." He took advantage of my call to tell me that he had finally created his Web site and that everyone can now learn Sango by clicking on http://sango.free.fr.

I took leave of Gilbert on a very hot night. I was already in a sweat when I got to his door, on the fourth floor of a walk-up apartment building. The air conditioning wasn't working. Not a breath of air was coming in the living room windows. Two young women were stretched out on couches. They barely greeted me. The heat discouraged the slightest movement.

I followed Gilbert into the kitchen and was dumbfounded to see that he was making *choucroute* in a pan heating on two burners at the same time. I told him I wouldn't be staying for dinner.

"Don't you think the girls are beautiful?"

"I didn't really look at them."

"Well, that was a mistake!"

He raised the lid off the pan, and a huge cloud escaped. Through the steam I detected his sniggering, which seemed almost diabolical to me.

"I find all of them sublime. I would gladly devote every hour of my life to watching naked girls go by. All the retired men in France should come here and spend their money on girls rather than wasting it on the races, the fools!"

I was suffocating. He unbuttoned his shirt. His stomach

was dripping with sweat. I took a beer from the fridge and drank from the bottle. It wasn't cold.

"Don't you feel younger here than in Paris?"

"I felt very young at one time. Then I began to get older. . . . I didn't get that much older, I just caught up to my age."

As soon as I arrived home, I called Alice, but I got her answering machine. I didn't leave a message.

Yves helped me to do a little shopping. I bought the bow and arrows for Jean's son, a fly swatter made of lion hair for Georges, two silver bracelets, one for Alice and one for Sandra, and a cat's head carved in bone for Paul-Marie Bourquin.

As we started on our rounds, Yves gave a few coins to a boy wearing a tattered purple shirt. An hour later, while I was paying for my purchases, I noticed the purple shirt among the people strolling in the artisans' quarter.

"Have you gotten used to Bangi?" Yves asked.

We had stopped at an outdoor café surrounded by a wooden fence.

"It's hard to remain a stranger in a city that uses the informal *tu* with you, one that calls you *baba*. I have the feeling I know more people here than in Paris. It's true that I've paid much more attention to people here than I ordinarily do in Paris or Athens."

"No doubt because you won't see them again. You look at them attentively because you won't be able to see them again. You become aware of their existence and say goodbye to them simultaneously."

The café owner, after having looked me up and down, asked me for an autograph. He had seen excerpts from my conference on television.

We talked about Gilbert.

"He has to go back to France for good in six months. From

then on he'll only be able to flirt with women his own age. He'll be quite unhappy."

"Do you think I could keep the blue pants and yellow shirt you lent me at the Youth Center? I'd like that."

There were gaps of a couple of centimeters between the planks of the wooden fence. I realized that an eye was staring at me through one of them. Yves recognized the child in the purple shirt at the same time I did. He was about to get up, but I held him back.

"I'm the one he's looking at. You already gave him money."

"It would certainly be easier to ignore misery if it were blind. But it has eyes and it looks at us."

We climbed the hill to fetch my bag and then brought it to the Air France office in the central city. Other passengers were checking their luggage. They moved wearily, almost with discouragement. It was as though their suitcases didn't belong to them, or as if they were disappointed that no black man was stepping forward to take charge of them. I was slightly uncomfortable among all these white people, as if I had stopped belonging to their group.

Yves will accompany me to the airport tomorrow night. I have no intention of asking him why he is afraid of nighttime. I think not asking him is the best way for me to express my respect for him.

On my last evening I ate alone at Couleur Café. The terrace was almost empty, perhaps because the orchestra was not performing. Vincent Sibierski turned his head away when he saw me. At ten o'clock, a power failure plunged the café and the adjacent streets into total darkness. Esther placed candles on the three or four tables that were occupied. Vincent Sibierski refused his.

Esther gave me her elephant hair bracelet as a gift. I was extremely moved by this, even though she asked me to send her a tee shirt, a sweat suit, and sneakers from Paris. She wears a size thirty-nine shoe.

I ate some threadfin fish, probably for the last time. I couldn't leave without saying goodbye to Sibierski. Finally he agreed to see me.

"Sit down," he said.

I could barely make out his face.

"You're a cabinetmaker?"

My question made his hackles rise.

"Why do you ask?"

"Because I just thought about the father of a friend of mine who came from Poland and had the same profession as you."

"Is he dead?"

"Probably. Did you ever live in Lille?'

"Is this some kind of interrogation you're subjecting me to?"

He was exaggerating his indignation to hide his curiosity.

"I can show you his name."

I placed my checkbook where Jean had written the name of his father in front of him and struck a match.

"Przybyszewski," he muttered. "I don't know any Przybyszewski. Strange name, don't you think?"

My disappointment overjoyed him, just as he had been overjoyed when he had showed me the ruins of the Studio de Paris. I put away my checkbook and left.

When I got home I found my father sitting in the middle of the steps of the wooden staircase. I had already seen him once in the same spot, at his house in Athens. His strength had abandoned him in the middle of the staircase.

"I won't read your letter. I am well aware that you are not the one who wrote it. And yet you wrote my name on the envelope. If you were so insistent that I read it, it's probably because you had something to tell me."

He seemed calm and relaxed.

"You didn't write the words that are in it, but its silence belongs to you. I don't know what kind of father you had, but mine as you know didn't like to talk much. In the end, it's just like you to leave me a silent letter to console me for your absence. You agree, don't you?"

My father was smiling.

"My publisher was right to tell me that this letter had something to do with me. The best proof of that is that I would be incapable of reading it: I would stop, like you did, at the third line."

I began climbing the steps. As I passed next to him, I brushed his face with the tip of my fingers.

Will I write something about Sango, in accordance with the wishes of the Alingbindo family? How could I pass over in silence this language that has kept me company for so long? I remember having said to Georges that novels always deal with a discovery. "Or a loss," he replied. One can easily evoke a discovery and a loss at the same time.

Languages return the interest you show in them. They tell you stories only to encourage you to tell your own. How could I have written in French if the language had not accepted me as I am?

Foreign words are compassionate. They are moved by the least little sentence you write in their language, and it doesn't matter if it's filled with mistakes.

I don't know how I'm going to begin, but I know I would like to end with foreign words. Wouldn't a story that begins in one language and ends in another be just typical of me?

Baba ti mbi a kui.

Mama na baba ti mbi a gue yekeyeke na wuruwuru pepe.

Mbi yeke gi mbi oko.

Mbi sara mbeti na faranzi, ngbangati so mbi yinga sango pepe.

Buku ti mbi awe.